A
MOOD
for
LOVE

Also by Mary Kenny:

Women Times Two: A Study of Working Mothers
Why Christianity Works
Abortion: The Whole Story
The Best of Mary Kenny (collected journalism)

A
MOOD
for
LOVE
AND OTHER STORIES

MARY
KENNY

Quartet Books
London   New York

First published by Quartet Books Limited 1989
A member of the Namara Group
27/29 Goodge Street, London W1P 1FD

Copyright © Mary Kenny 1989

British Library Cataloguing in Publication Data
Kenny, Mary
   A mood for love and other stories.
   I. Title
   823'.914 [F]

   ISBN 0-7043-2739-2

Typeset by AKM Associates (UK) Ltd, Southall, London
Printed and bound in Great Britain by
BPCC Hazell Books Ltd,
Member of BPCC Ltd, Aylesbury

Contents

Contents

A Mood for Love

It was a Monday when we set off – Zoe and I – to pay a visit to one of Budapest's most famous old spas. The Hungarian capital has the richest mineral deposits in Europe, and these produce deliciously hot springs – so excellent for one's health, don't you know. The November day was cold, raw: light snowflakes came drifting down, and the noonday air was white over the Danube.

This particular spa is located in a marvellous old hotel. Pure Hapsburg, pure Belle-Epoque. A great cliff rises behind the highly-decorated edifice, and a medieval castle, fronted by a statue of St Stephen – pure Crusader – sits atop the cliff. 'Can't you just imagine Edward VII coming here?' I said to Zoe, as we entered the marble hall that serves as a lobby, neo-classical statues all around us, aspidistras in the corners, if you please. 'Yeah,' said Zoe, sardonically, 'with several of his mistresses.' 'Pure decadence,' I murmured, as we queued up to pay for our entry tickets. 'No,' said Zoe, 'pure Communism. You have to come to a Communist country to get that real *fin-de-siècle* feeling.' At the desk, issuing tickets for the baths, sat a sullen *baboushka*, holding a cigarette with a very long finger of ash growing from its tip. Funny, I thought, you wouldn't see that in Western Europe – someone smoking in a health-spa. Quaint.

I love exotica, and what I especially adore about central Europe is all this weight of history, because life hasn't changed as much as it has in the West. This whole place was not only a relic of the Austro-Hungarian empire, but behind that old Hapsburg feeling was a sense of the Ottoman époque's shadow. Some of these old baths actually are relics from the period of Turkish occupation, and some of the pools have what I call harem-shaped windows – onion-shaped at the top.

Well, we stumbled through a variety of chambers, a pair of rather dumb tourists in the Hungarian vaporized air. Then, we were lucky enough to find a kindly, bossy little schoolteacher who spoke English and showed us where to go and what to do. We were ordered to take off all our clothes, and despatched, naked, towards the mineral-rich waters of the first pool. Naturally, this was the women's section of the spa – there was no mixed treatment here.

In the thermal pools we swam – no, dunked – in the soft, warm, soothing water. High-domed and misty with moist air, this stone and marble chamber was like a harem bath-scene painted by Ingres, or by Sir Lawrence Alma-Tadema; but the odalisques were long past desire. Most of the other women here were old: stout, wrinkled, worn out with life's worries and daily grind, arthritic, rheumatic and stiff in the joint. Their wispy hair was a dull grey and their old bosoms sagged in the water. Was it pensioners' day at the spa?

Zoe didn't pay any attention to the general nakedness – she is too sensible to give nudity a second thought. But the old women rather saddened me. 'This,' I thought, 'is what real women look like. This is what ordinary women look like.' People in Communist countries are less apt to be assaulted by commercial, idealized pictures of women – although that is beginning to change now, of course. Yet they seem more accepting of the plain, the ordinary, the *unvarnished* aspect of human flesh. It is as though, in the West, we feel we ought to aspire to look like something out of *Dallas*; whereas in less glossy lands, they accept the lumpen and the flawed side of human appearance. And yet it is not cheerful to face that ageing process which renders us all less aesthetic.

In a thermal bath, steam rises from the surface like a mysterious emanation; and if you are myopic as I am, the sensation of surrealist vision is enhanced.

Presently, a younger woman entered the pool near us, and as the vapoured air cleared a little, I could see she was a Venus among the crones. It was dramatic to notice the contrast: in the midst of all the droops and flabs and wrinkles and stretch-marks, here was a statuesque young goddess with a generous pair of breasts, which thrust forward proudly, full and firm. Her arms and legs were long and without a touch of wear and tear, *crêpe* or crinkle. Her face was sweetly, merrily, girlishly pretty, with a pert nose and green eyes.

Zoe and I were talking to one another about the silky feel of the water, the invigorating impact of the mineralized air around us. When she heard our conversation, the young Venus bobbed over towards us. 'Hi,' she said. 'It's a real pleasure to hear someone talk English.' We smiled to hear her American voice, and agreed that it had been awkward, puzzling over taps marked *Melegviz* and *Hidegviz* and trying to figure out which was hot and which was cold. It's not just *that*, she said. 'I'm a good linguist and can even make my way with inaccessible languages like Hungarian – it's that you get *lonely* for your mother-tongue if you are constantly talking in a foreign language. Don't you find that?'

Zoe explained that we were only in Hungary for six days; it was such a short break we didn't really mind. 'I see,' said the girl, agreeably. 'I live in Salzburg, in Austria, so I'm usually talking German. By the way, I'm Susy Joyce.' She clearly wanted to be friendly. Zoe introduced us both and explained that we lived in Edinburgh and tripping abroad was one of our little hobbies. Zoe likes new people, and responded to the girl's easy, open, Californian cordiality. And so Susy tagged along with us as we went through the procedures of the spa: the Turkish bath – in a silent fog, women stand around like still figures in a Fellini movie – and the plunge into ice-cold water thereafter. And then the return to the thermal spring-water again, in the marble pools with the cluster of grannies. And after that came the massage – a vigorous, medicinal business, without any of the caressing overtones of the erotic, as in the capitalist world.

In the Hungarian form of massage, strapping girls in white coats pumped the flesh of the female clients in the same mood as they might have served at a counter at Woolworths – talking guilelessly about the vicissitudes of everyday life with each other, across the bodies of their obediently inert customers.

Outside the massage cubicles – which wholly lacked privacy – a line of women awaited their turn on a bench. After some confusion over tickets, Susy got to the top of the queue straight away. The shrunken females sitting on the benches seemed to accept, almost automatically, as though it were part of the natural order, that this tall, straight, well-made American should take precedence over them, although it was obvious that she had jumped the queuing procedure. I watched her walk confidently into the massage cubicle, a very perfect physical specimen, and a prickling of resentment made itself felt. She fancies herself, I thought. She hadn't said two words to us, back in the thermal pool, before describing herself as 'a good linguist'. She was young, probably clever, and beautiful; she was also an American, with all the confidence imparted by the world's most dominant culture. What did they used to say about being born British? 'To have drawn the winning ticket in the lottery of life.' The Californian Princess, I thought, as I watched her, and watched the Hungarian women watching her, wistfully I thought, wonderingly, their little round shoulders in such contrast to her straight deportment.

As Susy stepped out of the massage room, she called over to Zoe and me – we were still awaiting our turn, too – to meet her later in the bar of the hotel. Would we? I was indifferent to this plan – pursuing the conversation with Susy was not a thought that engaged me – but Zoe, as usual, was all for being gregarious. Of course, she called back; it would be lovely. I made a face but Zoe took no notice whatsoever. I could think of better ways to spend the rest of the afternoon and evening.

It was past five o'clock in the afternoon, and the light was fading in the boulevards and over the high castellations of Budapest when Susy joined us in the intimate, plush little hotel bar. It was a snug little room off the main lobby, velvet and discreet.

Susy looked the picture of health as she settled into a corner. 'Wasn't that just marvellous?' she said, of the spa. 'I feel *great*! Don't you?'

'I feel *knackered*,' I said. I did. There was something about the spa experience that was emptying.

Susy hailed the barman authoritatively. He came over, saturnine, limpid-eyed, deferential. Susy and Zoe ordered vodka cocktails: in a fit of sudden Calvinism, I pointedly asked for soda water.

'Goodness gracious, I'm exhausted too,' Susy said, and then, glintingly wicked and saucy of eye, added, 'but then, I got no sleep last night.'

'Well, now!' said Zoe, as though talking to a clever child. 'Tell us more!'

'Yeah, well, I was in bed with someone!' Susy revealed, very pleased.

Zoe adores this kind of confidence. She's a doctor, and just can't get enough of hearing about other people's lives.

'No! A Hungarian? Everyone says they're so sexy!'

'No, not a Hungarian. A German, would you believe.' Susy sighed rather blissfully, a-flower with sexual fulfilment.

'There!' cried Zoe triumphantly, as though her faith in this bright prodigy had been justified. 'I can so identify! I've always had this *thing* for Germans! I call them my unfrocked SS men!' I hadn't heard this intelligence from Zoe before, though we had known each other since our twenties, over fifteen years ago. And her parents were Polish, Poles who had fled the Nazis. I was quite taken aback by this peculiar revelation – that she had a 'thing' for Germans.

'Kinda kinky, isn't it?' Susy sparkled. 'But he was great. Ardent! Never stopped. Can you imagine?' I could imagine. Only too well. Oh, my jealous spinster heart!

'He's got these piercing, crystal-blue eyes,' she went on dreamily.

The barman hovered and I paid for the drinks. That's right. Self-confident Californian ladies, I thought, expect other people to pay for their drinks, just as they expect to go first in a queue; those who expect royal treatment often get it, if only because others defer to their sheer self-confidence.

The bill, I noticed, came to over 400 Forints, which was, at the time, about a week's salary for many Hungarians. It was, naturally, a bar exclusively for foreigners.

Zoe isn't mean about sharing bills, but she was completely wrapped up in the younger girl's story. 'Blue, piercing eyes,' Zoe repeated Susy's words, with a romancing schoolgirl's look. 'They always have, those Germans – blue, piercing eyes!' Zoe was into heavy identification with Susy's fresh young sexual experience.

I was rather more sour about it all. Discomfort, embarrassment and jealousy mingled in my responses. I looked out over the darkening Danube and thought of the time . . . of another time, and another exotic place, and another romantic passion that had been mine. My turn for such episodes seemed to be over, and my reaction to the younger woman was not generous.

'His name is Boris,' Susy sipped away at her costly vodka. 'Funny, that, his having a Russian name. His mother was a ballerina, and she thought Russian names romantic.'

'*My* Germans were always called something like Manfred or Kurt or Ludwig,' giggled Zoe. 'The thing about them is, don't you agree, Susy? – that they're so correct and serious on their feet – it's all *gemeinschaft* and *gesellschaft* – and then it's such a contrast when you get them into bed!

'It's such a delight to find them so funny and tender and passionate, after all that po-faced stuff!' Well, curiouser and curiouser! Zoe had never told all this to me – and here she was, spilling it all out about 'my Germans' to this . . . randy little Miss Hotpants we seemed to have picked up.

I am sure I pursed my lips. I am sure I looked like the embittered spinster postmistress of village lore, moralizing about what she no longer has the opportunity to enjoy.

Susy told us how she had met Boris. She was staying at another hotel, in one of the main boulevards the other side of the Danube. It had been simple. She had been sitting alone, reading a book over dinner, trying to make her lone meal and her lone wine stretch over a couple of hours. Towards the end of the evening, as the hotel restaurant began to empty, she noticed a gregarious group still revelling in the corner. Presently, an older man from the group came over to her table – a little drunk, but rather gallant. He bowed and invited her to join their party. Susy speaks good enough German – she was living in Salzburg under some sort of sabbatical arrangement – and she was rather glad, even at this late stage, to be included in a little party. The older man seemed inoffensive, somehow.

By and by, the Hungarians in the group got up to go and Susy found herself alone with this elderly German, his son Boris, and an Italian man. They were all doing business in Budapest.

And so, said Susy, well, one thing led to another! She went on with the three men to a night club, where, she recalled, they drank Mumms Cordon Rouge champagne – at 2,000 Forints a bottle. A *month's* salary for many Hungarians, I noted disapprovingly. The older German grew too drunk; and the Italian could see that 'something was developing' between Boris and Susy. Pretty soon, Boris and Susy were back in his hotel, and it was bang, bang, bang all night long, until the dawn traffic broke in on her consciousness. Her body was sore from pleasure; her breasts, she told us voluntarily, felt black and blue from the effects of love-making.

Zoe thought this a perfectly thrilling tale, and almost applauded with encouragement as Susy caught her breath remembering the desire and its fulfilment. I must have looked as though I had sucked a lemon. I certainly felt lemony. The primitive, jealous female arose in my soul. The little trollope! – I reacted. Brazen! Shameless! Tart!

I didn't want to hear any more of Susy's story, indeed. I

didn't like the reaction in myself.

'Of course, he's married,' Susy said, then. 'There's always someone back home, isn't there? But I'm not bothered. It was just a great night of sex for me – nothing else. Really, nothing else at all.'

All the same, she examined her watch at this stage. He said he would telephone her at six o'clock, she explained. It was going to be his last night in Budapest. The following morning he was returning to Hanover, and to his wife. *Now* I bristled on behalf of the wife. The bitch! How could she prey on another woman's husband like this?

This was not a moral question which had greatly troubled me when I, like Susy, was 26. Morality had seemed to descend around my fortieth birthday.

'I guess,' Susy remarked, 'I guess I wouldn't be quite as uninhibited if I was back home. Hell, these guys probably took me for some kinda travelling prostitute. What a thought!' She made a face which faked discomfort.

I asked her what, in fact, her job was. She was an academic, she said. She taught ethics at a women's college. 'Not that I have any rigid moral concepts of right and wrong,' she added. 'These are relative terms, today. Value judgments are subjective. We have a non-structured, non-judgmental approach.' As a teacher myself, I was aware of this American fad for 'value-free' moral and cultural education, and I didn't have a high opinion of it. 'Non-judgmental' usually meant everyone just doing as they pleased, in my experience.

'Of course, I wasn't brought up with those views,' Susy explained, sipping the last part of her drink rather daintily. Goddammit, but she was pretty, and graceful too! 'I was raised as an old-fashioned Catholic. I'm half-Bavarian, half-Irish. But my Bavarian half – my mother – died when I was nine, and I figured, after that, religion could go screw itself.'

She said that in a way that implied a continuing hurt over the loss of her mother. I asked her if she had any Bavarian family still in Munich.

'Uh-huh,' she shook her head. 'Not in Munich. But I guess I

am trying to find the German part of my soul. If it exists. My soul, that is!'

Zoe suggested another round of drinks, but Susy declined. 'My father – that's my Irish half – developed a real problem with drink, after my mom passed on. He more or less went off his head with liquor, eventually. I got to be careful.'

Amazing how Americans always tell you the whole story of their lives – so *openly* – isn't it? I noticed Susy consult her watch, a little anxiously. She said she hoped that Boris would reach her all right, that it wasn't too confusing to have to track her down from her own hotel in Pest to this hotel bar in Buda. She had left a very clear message at her own hotel that she should be paged at the hotel of the spa.

'It's getting on for six,' Zoe remarked, preparing to make a tactful withdrawal. 'We'd better make tracks, Laura and I, anyway.'

Susy said there was no rush for us to go. If Boris were to telephone her, it would still take him another half an hour to come along over, from the other side of town. At the back of her mind too, I believe that she was calculating the possibility of a no-show from Boris. After all, a one-night stand is a one-night stand. Men always say they'll ring you the next day. It is the polite way of doing things. And if Boris were not to materialize ... then, I can imagine that Susy felt she might as well have the company of these mature British ladies for the evening, one of whom, at least, would be happy to discuss the pleasures and the rancours of the love game *ad infinitum*, providing motherly words of consolation about the faithlessness of the male.

Susy thought she would go on over to the reception desk anyhow, and just ask if there had been a call for her. But as she stepped outside the bar, and and through the saloon-type swing doors which separated it from the hotel lobby, there was a small exclamatory cry. We couldn't quite see what was happening, but we could hear. It sounded as if Boris was actually there – in the flesh. I even caught the words, spoken in English: 'Hello, pretty lady!' Oh, how seductive!

In a moment, Susy slipped back into the bar to fetch her

coat. Her face was alight with excitement, and relief too. He had more than kept his word to contact her: he had come for her! If Boris had arrived on a white steed, she could hardly have looked more like a gratified young demoiselle. A great night of sex? It meant much more, already.

Zoe handed her the coat, smiling broadly, almost lewdly. 'Have a great evening, my dear! Enjoy yourself! Bye!' Susy grinned back, and was gone. No question of introducing us to this Lohengrin: it would be like dragging forth a pair of middle-aged aunts.

As they passed through the hotel lobby together, the bar doors happened to open again, and we caught a glimpse of the pair. Boris was dark, tall, kind of skinny, with well-defined cheekbones and intense blue eyes. He wore a long leather coat – oh, frisson of kink! – tied tightly around his waist. His hand rested on Susy's buttock, tender yet proprietorial. The signal said: 'This, for here and now, is my woman. With my passion, I have branded her.'

When they were gone, Zoe left the snug bar and went over to the porter's desk to ring for a taxi. Then we waited for the car to arrive, thinking of Susy gasping with pleasure, all through the night, under this gorgeous Hun.

'There's something about a German in a leather coat!' Zoe shook her head in her just-fancy-that mode.

'You never told me about your weakness for the jackboot,' I said, rather sneeringly.

'Ach, I was only making conversation,' Zoe said lightly. 'Anyway, modern Germans aren't into jackboots, much. They're all shaggy guys with beards burbling on about the environment.'

'I wonder . . .' I said, and stopped. Speculating on Boris's sexual performance sounded prurient.

'Yes, I wonder what he's like between the sheets too!' Zoe agreed, and we laughed. 'But at our age, my dear – it's academic!' She laughed further, and I smiled unenthusiastically at this coda.

Night had fallen over the Danube as we rode back across

Szabadsag Bridge. Strange cities look wonderful by night, promising mystery and glamour. I looked at the lights along the river and thought, 'Susy will always remember Budapest.'

'He won't,' Zoe said later, when I spoke my thoughts. 'Boris will go home to his wife and make mad passionate love to *her* and pat his little children on the head, and soon he won't even remember Susy's name. Men are like that. It doesn't mean a thing.'

We were reflecting on the day's doings while eating a rather mournful supper at our hotel. It was a true Monday evening in the catering business. Dead. Even the Hungarian gypsy band couldn't work up a pretence of gaiety.

'I could scarcely forebear a stab of pure envy,' I confessed to Zoe, over the *ersatz* caviar. 'I *disapprove* of promiscuity, okay. I know it ends in tears, or VD, or abortions, or today, probably AIDS. But still. I couldn't help wishing terribly that I was twenty-six again, and that I had a body like that. It's so romantic, dammit – strangers in the night. A mood for love. There's a throwaway magic about a foreign romance. Ah,' I sighed. 'To feel that again!'

Zoe shook her head from side to side with that know-all wisdom of hers, which is both unsettling and irrefutable.

'I don't feel any envy,' she said convincingly. 'I am just pleased that people are still . . . well, just the way we were. That AIDS hasn't, after all, put a stop to the glorious brief romance. I remember two nights in Vienna twenty years ago. He was a French lawyer called Antoine. It was perfect. In forty-eight hours you have just enough time to see the best of one another, to enjoy a sense of love suffused with delight because it's a gossamer thing . . .

'And when he was gone, I wandered around the city in a romantic daze, thinking – "This is where we were together, and here and here and here." The whole city was filled with a poignant eroticism for me – and more than eroticism: enchantment, which is better. It was long ago, now, before the children were born, before Freddie came and then went. But I still remember.'

11

Zoe looked thoughtful, philosophical, her usually animated face composed. She took a draught from the Mount Badacsony wine we had ordered ('a decaying version of a once virile wine' said my gastronomic guidebook) and went on calmly . . . 'I still remember, indeed. I'm not bitter. I'm not envious. It's wrong to be greedy. And the sex urge passes with age, you know. Nature isn't interested in getting us worked up once we're on course for the menopause. It doesn't serve her purpose. Anthropologically, we should be grandmothers by now. I'll be fifty next month, remember. And you know, Laura, in time you come to see the joys of celibacy. A single bed becomes welcoming. You accept.'

I sighed some more and passed on to the Olasz Reisling, dismissively described by my gastronomic expert as 'a withered shadow of a wine that was once alluring and girlish in other places, other times'. I didn't accept what Zoe said. Not yet. And I didn't like the idea that inevitably I would have to.

Yet I knew I would be forced to accept, sooner or later – and probably sooner – that life passes; that you say goodbye to the young, foolish things; that the opportunity and the nerve fail, and finally desire is no longer aroused as the spoor of attraction falters. When you are young, you have a future. It is in this future that you offer this promise, this possibility, when you become involved with a lover. When you are middle-aged, that future is half-spent, and perhaps the most vivid parts of it are over. Old people do not remember their middle-age very much; they remember the young years, when everything was fresh, and impressions were greatest.

Zoe was indeed being wise, as she usually is. Romance is the constituency of the young. Afterwards the pleasures come from remembering. As night closed in on Budapest, I felt a gloomy sense of time gone by.

Zoe and Susy had exchanged addresses during the course of chattering about Boris, and as it happened, Susy sent her a note two months later.

Zoe had scrawled a few words to me about Susy's progress on a postcard accompanying some snaps she had taken in Hungary. 'It seems that Susy and Boris are still an item,' she wrote. With this intelligence, my sense of envious discomfort was rekindled with a sudden flame. So it wasn't a one-night stand, after all! The bitch had prospered from it!

Yet wait: read on. 'There is *trouble in Paradise* just the same. There are problems, and unhappiness. But then it always was notoriously difficult for Germans to enter the Elysian Fields.'

I thought I garnered just a glance of malice in Zoe's words. I hoped I did. We would not be human without a little envy and malice – as the Germans themselves say, *schadenfreude*: being pleased when things go wrong for others. I smiled at Zoe's words: 'Trouble in Paradise' – eh? I'll drink to that!

A Change of Life

There comes a moment in every woman's life when she wants a
change. 'I am bored with my life – I think I'll have an affair,'
writes the weary housewife to the agony aunt. And the wise
agony aunt (if such a character exists) replies: 'What you need,
my dear, is a change, not a disaster. Aren't there any interesting
evening classes in your neighbourhood!'

Some women take up learning Spanish, to be sure, only to
find that the evening class is full of other women who cannot
tell a double negative from a plural noun – in English, that is –
but who have nonetheless been linguistically inspired by an
experience on the Costa Brava. Others take to dieting, because
they want to become new women, a notion that husbands find
justifiably suspicious, since *they* do not wish to become new
men, and a fat wife is a more secure possession than a thin one.
A few find religion, or feminism, or some other ism currently in
vogue – politics, like frocks, are largely a matter of fashion.
Margaret Duffy, being an exceptionally quiet and serene
woman decided, at the age of forty-seven, simply to give up
smoking. This was hardly a world-shaking decision, but it
happened to signal a turning-point.

As is so frequently the case, the reason why she made this
resolve arose from a poignant moment in life's passage. The
idea of quitting cigarettes – seriously – had occurred to her at
the time of her mother's death, when Margaret was forty-
six. Margaret's mother had been feeble and geriatric, and

mildly demented, and when she came to visit Margaret in West Hampstead (it was called Kilburn in 1961, when Margaret and her husband had first bought their pleasant Edwardian house there for £6,000) she needed a lot of care and attention.

Margaret's mother was given to drinking ink, supposing it to be a sweet liqueur, and to lighting the gas under the electric kettle, on the theory that all kettles needed gas under them, which had been the case in her own household. And then, when the old lady had died in Ireland, at the age of eighty-one, Margaret had experienced this queasy sense of nakedness before the forces of time and decay.

'I'm next in line,' she thought as she watched the coffin lowered into the clay, on a grey morning, beneath the darkening Dublin mountains. And her sister, three years younger, had remarked: '*We* are the older generation now.' Morbidly, the sister had gone on to remark that there was space yet in the burial place for several more family members. But then, ever since Ann had been widowed herself, she had developed this macabre turn of mind.

I *must* stop smoking, thought Margaret. Cigarettes will be the death of me. When things calm down a bit.

But there is never a right time in life to make a difficult decision. See how modern young women agonise over the choice of having a baby. But if not now, when? And if a decision is forever deferred, is the will not lacking? Margaret found it endlessly awkward trying to create a window of peace and tranquillity in which to abandon her loyal friend, ally and stalwart companion, the cigarette.

The children were leaving home – her son Peter to attend a seminary in Rome, her daughter Nuala to become a student nurse in a Leeds teaching hospital – all of which propelled Margaret into a state of suppressed anxiety. Margaret's outward serenity and stable, ordered ways hid deep insecurities and a propensity to worry about small things, even to succumb to an attack of migraine when overwhelmed with worry and fear. And when she took up a part-time job with the local authority, well, that threw her into a whirl of anxiety. Fearing she would not be able to cope, she doubled her cigarette intake, starting with the post-breakfast ciggie. Then, finding she was more than able for the job, she would relax with a cigarette.

Then she turned forty-seven and began reading articles in magazines about the menopause – *that* change of life – and the urgent need for hormone replacement therapy. The very thought of this had Margaret reaching for the comfort of a Silk Cut. And then she noticed that Mark seemed to be getting increasingly morose in his ways, and she worried if he was quite well. *He* worried about his health, too – his father had died of heart disease in his fifties, and this caused Mark to brood moodily. He fussed petulantly about a low-fat diet and monitored his blood pressure carefully.

'I thought you were going to give up the fags,' her husband remarked one evening as Margaret sat in the kitchen over a cup of tea and a post-supper smoke.

'Actually, I've been thinking of attending an anti-smoking clinic,' she said, a little hesitantly. There had been an advertisement on the notice-board at work for an organization which helps smokers quit. Still, Margaret knew that Mark was against all such measures. He was virulently critical of all 'counselling', 'support groups', 'interface communications', all new-fangled, American-inspired gobbledegook; all psychologists, sociologists and the whole breed of shrinks. He was overwhelmed by such phenomena, and references to such by the younger and more radical members of the teaching profession, and it represented, to him, all that had caused educational and moral standards to decline.

'Fairly good codswallop, I'd say,' he remarked coolly, opening the weekly edition of his Irish newspaper. 'If you want to stop smoking, why can't you just stop, like I did? Why do you want to go and bare your soul to a lot of other neurotics talking a lot of post-Freudian balderdash?'

Margaret tried to explain that it was just a way of getting

17

support from other people in the same boat; giving up smoking was very hard for her. She couldn't do it alone.

'I recently read in a magazine that giving up cigarettes is harder than giving up heroin,' she told him.

'Ah, you read too much rubbish in these women's magazines,' he replied scornfully. 'They're produced by the self-same dirt-birds and con-men that have brought about the wholesale collapse of modern society.'

Mark went on some more about half-baked modern ideas replacing a bit of much-needed backbone and moral fibre. Margaret didn't argue with him, because she knew the location of Mark's emotional bruises and feelings of failure. She had seen him go into teaching as a shining idealist, full of commitment to education having the power to change the world and bring better opportunities to all; and she had seen him gradually worn down by the system, by the administration, by trade-union trouble-making, by children who had been taught to despise learning before they had the chance to learn, by a culture which admired philistine vulgarity, greed, stupidity and casual pornography.

The radical young teachers and educationalists in the borough where he taught, with their witch-hunts on behalf of 'anti-racism', their malign, Marxist perceptions of Irish politics, their attacks on class discipline in favour of a self-indulgent cult of ignorance masquerading as 'self-expression' and 'creativity', had all contributed to his bitterness. Margaret understood all this, because she knew him all too well. But she was finding Mark increasingly difficult to live with.

He had been so thoughtful and considerate, too, when she had first known him – his quiet kindness was what first attracted her. His introverted streak, a certain shyness expressed through sidelong glances, had seemed charming after the brash leering of other young men, their lunging passes and maladroit fumblings in the course of a dance or a walk home from a party. Mark, in contrast, had been every inch a gentleman. But as characteristics often become emphasized with age, so his introverted streak had turned to melancholy, his thoughtfulness had taken a critical, negative aspect, his shyness had become bleak.

'Please yourself, of course,' he ended, with a wry, resigned smile 'It might do you good to meet a different class of person, I suppose.'

Margaret did think to herself that it might indeed do her good to get away from the silent house of an evening.

The anti-smoking clinic took place on a Monday night and was held in an Islington health centre. Margaret took the tube to Baker Street and then mounted a bus, promising herself one last fag on the top deck. It was a purple, mild September evening, and London had that look of promising expectation that cities wear before the theatres start. At such moments, Margaret allowed herself to wonder what it might be like to be young again, to be single, to be without responsibilities, to be unyoked from marriage. By any measure, Margaret's marriage had been a success. But it had lasted some twenty-five years, and after a quarter of a century, a person might be forgiven for yearning for a life-change.

The session turned out to be disappointing. Margaret had hoped that it might be confessional, open, vivid, full of interesting characters revealing confidences and telling anguished stories about their struggle with nicotine. But it was stiff and intimidating. There was a bossy, talkative Welsh doctor in a white coat who harangued the group, bombarding them with repulsive X-ray pictures of diseased lungs, hearts, throats and bronchii. Instead of being invited to tell their sins, the people in the group were admonished for committing them. Instead of being offered healing through truth-telling, they were shown the punishment that awaited them if they persisted in their wrong-doing. Just as sinners were once given glimpses of hell for their misdeameanours, these smokers were being given evidence of the physical rot that would corrupt their bodies in the here and now.

Dr Williams' exhortatory speech echoed James Joyce's

famous account of the damnation to come: see the living skeletons with cancer, the men with gangrene slowly eating up their legs, the women whose reproductive organs were polluted with filth, the utter filth, of tobacco. Margaret felt browbeaten.

There was an interval, with tea and plain biscuits, as the group, looking chastened, chatted timidly.

'Are you a heavy smoker?' Margaret ventured to ask the woman seated next to her, a delicate, dark creature whose hair was drawn back in a ballerina style.

'You bet!' the woman replied, unperturbed. 'Two packs a day! But I'm still not sure if I'm *motivated* to quit. Are you?' Her accent was, Margaret thought, English, with some kind of American overlay.

'All the information makes me feel guilty,' Margaret admitted apologetically. 'And I really do want to give it up. But I still can't help looking on the cigarette as a friend.' A packet was asleep in her handbag, lying in wait should its ministrations be urgently required.

'Apart from killing you, a cigarette is a good friend,' the dark girl replied, wisecracking. 'Unlike other friends, it never makes any other demands.'

'What do you think of the doctor?' Margaret asked her.

'Creep!' the woman replied out of the side of her mouth. 'Wanker!' she added, for good measure.

With that, Dr Williams resumed the meeting, and his flow of invective began again.

Still, despite the fearsomeness of the tactics used, Margaret determined, on her way home, to start fighting her need to smoke in earnest. Every time the urge arose, she would think of the diseased organs. She would imagine dying slowly and breathlessly from emphysema, or picture an abrasion on her lung being rubbed and rubbed until it turned into a tumour, like Dr Williams had said.

Mark was asleep in front of the flickering TV set when Margaret got in. She poured herself a small whisky – a nightcap they usually took together – and was about to waken him gently when the telephone rang.

It was her sister-in-law, Sheila, in Birmingham. Could Margaret give a bed to Cousin Anna, the nun, who was passing through London on her way home from the Philippines? Cousin Anna had done some wonderful work in the Third World, Sheila mentioned. Cousin Anna, Margaret knew, would also expect to be waited on; she was wonderful in the Third World, largely because she ran her missions like a Victorian District Commissioner – with commanding presence. She would not be an easy guest, but of course Margaret would not refuse to look after such an exemplar of Christian altruism. How long would she want to stay? Well, she'd be on her way to Ireland, but it would be nice for her to relax in London for a week or ten days, wouldn't it? Margaret nodded in agreement, sighed imperceptibly, and reached for a cigarette.

It was to be two more Mondays before Margaret got a chance to return to the anti-smoking clinic. One Monday, she had been crippled with migraine. The following Monday she had had to take Cousin Anna down to Eastbourne to visit an elderly aunt there. A mother is, after all, responsible for guests and elderly relatives as much as for offspring!

Margaret had managed to reduce her cigarette intake somewhat – she was down to less than a full packet a day. And when she got to the group session, she told this to Dr Williams, expecting some encouragement for her achievement.

'A packet of cigarettes a day!' he thundered. 'Twenty cigarettes *per diem*! A score of coffin-nails the better to seal your hearse! That won't do at all, young lady!' At forty-seven, Margaret wasn't sure whether being called 'young lady' was complimentary or patronizing, but she blushed with embarrassment anyhow. 'Do you realize what a packet of death-delivering cigarettes do to your body and your brain each day?' And he was off again, in declamatory pulpit style. This time the comparison was not so much with a Joycean Jesuit as with a Wesleyan preacher of the 19th century. He harped much on the impurity of the fag, on the way it left a stain on the character and on the person, on the dark corruption, and on the shadow of wrongdoing conjured up by the offence of pulling on a smoke.

Margaret listened to Dr Williams, and thought how right he was all the same, and how she had begun to hate herself for the sins she had committed, from weakness, with the malevolent fag. The genie that had been her friend and protector was now being transformed into a Satanic figure, whose head was smoke and sulphur, and whose hooves were butts elongated with ash droppings. *Get thee behind me*: she closed her eyes and wished the Evil One away. But still the packet lay in her handbag, just as an idea, just in case.

As Margaret emerged into the sharper October air, the woman with the ballerina hairstyle fell into step next to her. 'How have you been getting along?' she asked Margaret in a friendly voice.

Margaret grinned ruefully. 'I'm not a good girl, you know,' she sighed. 'I'm so weak about it.'

The lights of Islington's Upper Street blazed gregariously. The fine Georgian church of St Mary's was warmly lit from inside its Palladian front porch.

'Now – no backsliding! Conjure up some nice repulsive disease before your eyes!' the other woman cried, in a sardonic caricature of Dr Williams. 'Say,' she added spontaneously, 'do you feel like a drink? There's a very decent wine bar just up here on the left.' Margaret felt very much like a drink indeed, now that the invitation had been proffered. The anti-cigarette fight was getting her down. She couldn't remember when she had last felt such a sense of depression.

'Just the ticket,' she told the other woman, and they turned into Almeida Street together.

Margaret was not the generation – or even the type – of woman who would feel entirely comfortable going into a strange pub alone or with another woman. But a wine bar was different.

It was panelled in wood, with lively, radical posters on the walls oddly in contrast to its atmosphere of bourgeois gentility; young women with short hair and very red lipstick, looking like absconding innocent schoolgirls, acted as waitresses.

Margaret's companion introduced herself as Judy Rosenthal. She was a crisp, decisive little person. She was the sort, Margaret could well imagine, who did not waste time humming and hawing or letting herself be put upon. You could see by her manner and her conversation that she was self-assured.

Judy was talkative, too. She described herself as a business-woman – she ran her own small business supplying educational medical aids to overseas countries, plastic pieces of human anatomy used in medical schools and the like. She was also interested in setting up self-help groups for women to help them overcome addictions of various kinds – Judy had done some psycho-sexual counselling in the United States. And she was thinking of going into politics at some stage too. She was married, although, she explained, she and her husband had a contract for an 'autonomous and independent lifestyle'. They were also childless 'by choice'.

Just the sort of person, Margaret reflected, that Mark would most disapprove of: all that American psycho stuff, all that counselling and jargon.

Still, Judy seemed good company, and was of an optimistic frame of mind, which cheered up Margaret. So did the two glasses of Gewurtztraminer.

Margaret fell into the habit of having a glass of wine or two – or sometimes three – with Judy Rosenthal on a Monday evening after that. And just as Dr Williams was seeking to convert his listeners to the gospel of non-smoking – and probably succeeding, with the majority – Margaret realized that Judy, too, had something to preach. Judy was a post-feminist feminist; not strident and left-wing like some of Mark's younger teacher colleagues, but affirmative, indi-vidualistic and very keen on capitalism. 'It's great to make money,' Judy would say. 'It's great to get people in to help you. That's not exploitation – that's economic development.' Judy thought trade unions 'negative' – her favourite put-down word. They bred 'dependency'. Judy was very critical about dependency of any kind.

Her marriage was the weirdest that Margaret had ever come across. She and her husband David shared a house in Clapham. He lived upstairs and she lived downstairs. They sometimes met for meals, and sometimes even slept together, but there was a strict pact of 'autonomy' accorded to each partner.

'Married people, or partners of any kind, should not be enslaved to one another,' Judy said. 'Domesticity on the old model is primitive. It is ridiculous for a grown woman to spend her time, her energy, her best years shopping and cooking and cleaning up after a man. It is denying a woman her own autonomy. Denying her a life of her own, fulfilment, culture. Women should not be forced to spend their lives servicing other people's needs, as they still do in so much of the world.'

Margaret was impressed by some of this thinking. She hadn't cared for the 'all-men-are-rapists' feminism among the boiler-suited activists in the local authority offices, but Judy was saying something she could feel an echo of in her own life. Though, of course, she had misgivings.

'But . . .' she began. 'When children are young, they need care. When people are old, they need care. When someone in the family is sick, they need care. Someone has to do it.'

'Why does it always have to be women?' Judy asked sharply. 'People should learn to take more responsibility for their own lives. If you bring a child into the world, sure, you should care for it together until it reaches independence. But once a child can exercise autonomy, I don't see any further reason to perpetuate the family links. And old people should either make provision for their declining years, or have the decency to end their own lives with dignity.'

Margaret looked at Judy wide-eyed. She had never met anyone like Judy before – who came out with such startling statements so coolly.

24

Judy then started to talk about a weird-sounding tribe in Africa called the Ik, who, Judy said, had developed an admirably sensible attitude towards survival and autonomy. Caring for tribal members who could not survive on their own was rejected by the Ik as ill-adapted behaviour. Among the Ik, individuals were not allowed to become a drain on others, because it was ruinous of energy and food sources for people to be dependent. Judy clearly admired the Ik.

'So if your husband becomes an invalid, you must make your choices,' Judy told her. 'If you choose to give up twenty, twenty-five years of your prime of life, then that's what you choose. If you don't want to do it, though, *don't* do it. Don't martyrize yourself and don't be blackmailed. Sell your house and check him into professional care. Overdose him if you can get away with it. I know this sounds tough, but it's just not fair that a woman who has spent a quarter of her life looking after her family should spend the next quarter as a nurse-maid. You only have one life to lead, Margaret!'

Margaret remembered an advertisement from years ago which proclaimed – 'If I only have one life, let me live it as a blonde!' It struck her then as a pagan sort of notion. Catholics were taught that this life was but a rehearsal for the next one; what mattered was the judgment in the hereafter. But at forty-seven, with the sand falling through the hour-glass ever quicker, Margaret felt a little pressed, somehow. Whatever this present life was, rehearsal or not, it should be savoured to one's best ability. Whatever was to follow could take care of itself.

She was a little tipsy going home that evening, she knew. The lights of Islington were shinier than ever, and looking at them, it seemed as though each street lamp was ringed with a brilliant halo.

Christmas was coming, and there was so much to do. The cards, the presents, the cooking and shopping and wrapping and decorating and getting and spending. It's not the *thought* that counts, Margaret said to herself as she battled through

Boots' gift department. It's the money and the time and the carrying home in the rain, and the careful sealing in fancy paper and sellotape and migraines you have gone through in the hunt for appropriate presents. Margaret ritually took all the Christmas chores on herself. She never asked Mark to help, and he, being an Irishman of the old school, or perhaps just being a man who had always been serviced in these matters, seldom thought to offer.

Peter, their son, was staying on in Rome for Christmas itself, but hoped to come home for a visit early in the New Year. Nuala, their daughter, was returning, and there was a boyfriend in tow, too.

'The bad news, Mum, is that he's black,' Nuala told her cheerfully over the telephone. 'The good news is that he's a Catholic.' Margaret was not particularly worried about either of these aspects of the visitor. What actually perturbed her were the sleeping arrangements that must be organized. She could not bring herself to offer her unmarried 19-year-old daughter a conjugal bed; and yet, the way that young people were nowadays, they were bound to be sharing one, weren't they? Margaret fretted over this until she got a headache.

Things were busy for her at work as well, and her boss asked Margaret if she would like to increase her commitment to a four-day week. Although the borough complained unceasingly about the beastly cuts imposed by the heartless Tory Government, there always seemed to be plenty of work for someone like Margaret who, in her old-fashioned way, could spell, type correctly, take a neat short-hand note and was methodical about office management.

Margaret dropped out of the Monday evening sessions at the anti-smoking clinic at this period in the run-up to Christmas, because there just wasn't time. She was still struggling against the cigarette urge – she had read it would take six months, at least – but she was doing quite well. Even when the cat, whom Margaret was fond of, got a horrible dose of cat flu and had to be put down, Margaret did not yield to a cigarette, though the occasion made her feel most forlorn.

26

However, she did ring Judy Rosenthal – as her designated 'therapy support partner' – for a chat about the struggle against nicotine. She asked Judy how she was getting along without smoking.

'Actually, terrific,' Judy said, enthusiastically. 'But then a funny thing has happened to me. I'm pregnant.'

'That's lovely, Judy,' Margaret responded, genuinely pleased. Judy was younger than her, of course – maybe in her middle to late thirties.

'Of course,' Judy went on conversationally. 'We haven't decided whether we're going to continue the pregnancy or not. It wasn't planned, which means the pregnancy hasn't really occurred with our full voluntary consent.'

'Nature doesn't always seek consent for these things,' Margaret said, with a sardonic inflexion.

'Right!' agreed Judy cheerfully. 'So we're considering whether to terminate the pregnancy or continue. In a way, it's an interesting development because it gives us a concrete choice, rather than a theoretical one.'

'I see,' said Margaret. After Judy's colloquy about the cold-blooded ways of the Ik, this line of thinking did not really surprise her. On an impulse, Margaret decided to be affirmative herself. If not now, when?

'I'm sure you'll enjoy having a baby,' she said. 'It's the ultimate growth experience, after all. No pun intended,' she added lamely.

'Sure thing,' said Judy. 'I'm starting to think that way too. Anyway, it's a great way to quit smoking! The urge just goes!'

Margaret remembered that all too well, and felt a pang of menopausal broodiness.

'You're just beginning the best years of your life, Judy,' she said, a little wistfully. She remembered Peter and Nuala as babies: they smelled so gorgeous.

'You make it sound really positive, Margaret,' said Judy. 'I like that positive thinking! Though I guess it would entail a certain amount of adjustment – a change of lifestyle.'

You can say that again, Margaret thought. You can say

goodbye to all those fancy ideas about 'autonomy', probably forever, she warned Judy mentally. But her natural prudence restrained her from voicing these thoughts. All mothers like to see their race increased. Join the club. See what it's really like up here in the front line, sister! So all she said was: 'Yes, Judy, but everyone needs a change of life every now and then, don't they?'

Christmas came, and Mark fussed ever more about not eating this and not eating that, and feeling his chest with self-regarding hypochondriasis. Margaret worried about him ever more; it was clear that her husband was either on the road to a chronic heart condition or to chronic, self-obsessed cur-mudgeonliness. She didn't know which was worse.

Nuala and the boyfriend arrived. They behaved with impeccable discretion and kept to their single beds, never mentioning the matter of sharing. Margaret had no way of knowing whether they normally shared a bed or not, and she was relieved indeed to be left in ignorance. You never knew with young people, of course; and the boy, whose mother was Irish, whose father was Caribbean, and who was pure Lancashire all the same, was of a serious, religious cast of mind.

Margaret now wondered why she had worried so much about such a triviality, instead of trusting her sensible, and sensitive, daughter. Still, the stress headaches did not disappear.

On Boxing Day – or St Stephens's Day, as they still called it, in the Irish custom – Frank and Sheila came down from Birmingham, and there was another meal to be concocted. And on December 28, just before Nuala and the boyfriend were due to go back North, Margaret celebrated her 48th birthday. A surprise cake was produced, with a jumble of candles atop the blue and white icing.

'You'll have the breath now to blow them out, Mum,' Nuala said. She was proud that her mother had stopped smoking.

The candles, Margaret noted, had a haze of coloured haloes

around their lighted tips, and as she drew breath to blow upon them, she felt a shooting pain in her left eye, piercing through her head. She put her hand up to her forehead, dazed with this sense of pain, which was quickly followed by nausea and a desire to vomit. 'Oh Jesus,' she moaned. 'Oh God. Oh Jesus, Mary and Joseph, I feel so sick.'

There was a commotion as Nuala took her mother to the bathroom, and helped her through a miserable vomiting session. And then the daughter took the mother into her own bedroom, where Margaret lay down with a feeling of exhaustion.

It was Mark, actually, who decided to call a doctor, when the pain over Margaret's eyes continued episodically. This was not to be the local GP, but a private medical arrangement that Mark had entered into for both of them, anticipating a sudden illness himself. (So this was how Mark was spending the small legacy his Aunt Maureen had left him – in buying extra medical care. It showed how much the matter had concerned him.)

The young doctor arrived, and asked Margaret to close her eyes so that he might touch her eyeballs. He asked her some questions about headaches and migraines. He asked her if she saw haloes ringed around lights – street lights, church candles, any lights. Mark came and sat with her the while, holding her hand. And once again he seemed the kindly, considerate young man she had fallen in love with. The middle-aged curmudgeon had quite disappeared.

With remarkable speed, Margaret found herself referred to an eye hospital in Clerkenwell, and subjected to more tests. Within a dramatically short space of time, she was informed that she had developed glaucoma, and would almost certainly become blind.

She found it hard to take this in, at first. Surely glaucoma was something affecting poor river folk in Africa – perhaps people like Judy's friends, the Ik? The consultant, Mr Bhagat, explained that many thousands of people in the developed world get glaucoma each year, and lose their sight in consequence. 'We will, of course, be doing everything we can to save your sight,' he said, in his courteous Indian phrasing. 'There is so much progress going on with this disability now. But you will have to adapt your life somewhat, all the same. Is your husband helpful?'

'He can be,' Margaret said. Mark had been so wonderful since this shock had struck. So sweet, so thoughtful, and so oddly cheerful again. Not thinking about himself was doing him a power of good. Perhaps, too, he needed to be needed. Perhaps he had worried about being a burden to her, if he had become ill, and he was gratified that, on the contrary, he could look after her while he had his health at least.

'That is good, that he is helpful to you,' Mr Bhagat told her. 'You will need him by your side in the coming times. It's important to have someone who can care for you in these circumstances.'

Margaret was still in a state of shock and half-belief. She was horrified at the prospect of losing her sight, although she cherished the glimmer of hope which the doctors had left her. She also felt profoundly grateful to her husband, and her family, who had all been so wonderful to her. Her heart melted at the thought of them, and this wave of warmth after all the anxiety made her feel peculiarly light-headed and irresponsible.

She fixed an imperfect gaze on Mr Bhagat. 'You'll kill me for this,' she said. 'But I would like to smoke a cigarette.' What the hell, she thought. I am going to ask for what I want, after all.

'I thought you would,' the doctor replied. 'And so did your husband. We frown on these things in hospitals, but I'm going to break the rules.' He opened a drawer and took out a packet with the familiar purple and white format. Mark had clearly provided them, just in case.

Margaret drew on the fag, banishing all guilt. 'I've stopped before and I'll stop again, but just for now, I am permitting myself the indulgence.' Then, *à propos* of nothing, she added: 'By the way, have you ever heard of an East African tribe called the Ik?'

Mr Bhagat put his hand to his chin thoughtfully. 'Yes,' he said. 'Yes, I have. Not in a medical context, particularly. But there is a famous anthropological study about them. They died out, in the end, because they were so disagreeable to one another. They developed such ferocious techniques for individual survival that they overlooked the importance of altruism, of what you might call mutual support. Yes, a fascinating study. Have you been interested in anthropology, Mrs Duffy?'

Margaret was smiling, shaking her head from side to side, as though in wonder, and then laughing with great merriment, throwing her head back heartily at the thought of some drollery. 'Autonomy and the Ik!' she laughed. 'Autonomy and the Ik! Wait until I tell a thoroughly pregnant Judy Rosenthal!' Then she looked up at the medic again: 'Don't worry about my having to adapt to my condition. I was expecting a change of life anyhow. Now I'm getting two for the price of one!' And she started laughing hysterically again.

Mr Bhagat looked at his patient with some surprise. She seemed to have something of a volatile personality, he thought. Fortunate that she was so thoroughly supported by a stable family. Very fortunate indeed.

A Marriage is Dissolved

Who knows, really, what makes a marriage work? Who knows, really, what causes it to fall asunder? For all the in-depth studies that have been done on marriage itself, it still remains a mystery to those most intimately involved. Especially when it fails.

It surprised me to glimpse Xan O'Hara at the Oxford conference that I was attending on the future of nuclear energy. It surprised me because the conference was organized by the ecology group to which I belong: the sort of people that Xan would have regarded as cranky lefties. Yet there he was, large as life, standing in the seventeenth-century bar adjacent to the college which hosted the affair. Large as life, slightly drunk, and very much alone.

I didn't think that he would recognize me. He had been a friend – well, perhaps the word is a 'colleague' – of my late husband, and he had only known me glancingly, back in the 1960s and 70s. So I went over and introduced myself, as it were. I always introduce myself, as I have the kind of face that people seem to forget quite easily. 'Hello, Xan,' I said. 'I'm Ann Bellinger, Roger's wife.' Even after five years, I find it difficult to say the word 'widow'.

He turned a brown, unsteady eye towards me. 'Well, well, as I live and breathe!' he declared. He smiled, and with an exaggerated gallantry, kissed my hand. 'After all these years!' He was carelessly dressed and had put on weight. I was carefully dressed, and had grown thinner. People change, in middle life.

'Have a drink!' he said, invitingly. 'I only come here for the beer! No other reason,' he lowered his voice, 'to be in such a dump. Such weirdoes!' The room was panelled in oak, and though picturesque, was not comfortable. The clientele were a wholesome-looking crowd.

'Thanks,' I said cheerfully. 'I'll have whatever fizzy water they offer here. I'm driving back to London tonight.'

'Ever the cautious Annie!' he responded, in a tweaking, faintly mocking way.

Xan was, I remembered, the kind of man who believed in living dangerously, and he regarded me as the kind of woman who would disapprove of risk, although that was not entirely the case. Perhaps his judgment of my character was not unconnected with an insignificant episode years ago, when I had politely repudiated a casual pass he had made at me. He thought I was too unadventurous, whereas I thought, even in the swinging sixties, that adultery is bad for marriage. Now he probably scarcely remembered that moment of desire, but I guessed he would have registered me as some kind of stick-in-the-mud.

He brought me a Perrier and we sat down on one of the wooden benches which seemed remarkably like a particularly punishing church pew – designed for penitents who liked to suffer at prayer. He was drinking beer with a chaser of whisky, that Scots combination for the hard man who wants maximum intoxication in the quenching of thirst, seeking oblivion before the pubs shut. Yet it was only seven o'clock on a bright April evening.

'Cheers!' he gave the toast. 'How are tricks?'

'Okay, thanks,' I said, and left it at that.

Then he remembered.

'Frightfully sorry about Rodge,' he murmured, referring to my husband's death. 'Rotten business. I was in South

America when I heard.'

I said nothing for a moment, and then responded quietly: 'Yes, we miss him.'

Xan clearly didn't want to get involved in a macabre conversation about the dead – nobody does, I notice, and he turned his gaze towards the bearded organic-looking souls around us.

'What are you doing with this lot?'

'I've joined an ecology group,' I explained. 'We're campaigning against nuclear power.'

'Bunch of nutcases,' he smiled, taking out a cigarette – a rare commodity in the company we were in. 'Nuclear fuel is the most useful invention since sliced bread. Hell of a lot safer – and cleaner – than coal.'

I don't like personal arguments, so I didn't exactly contradict Xan. All I said, evenly, was, 'I believe the facts show otherwise, but of course, everyone is entitled to their opinion.'

'I remember now what struck me most about you,' Xan smiled, with a note of boyish wickedness. 'So bloody tolerant. So bloody English.' He drew on his cigarette, and looked away. There was regret, now, in his well-made face. 'Still, maybe there's a lot to be said for tolerance. Perhaps I should have had a bit more of it in my life.'

'How is Vanessa?' I asked after his wife.

He made a waving gesture with his hand. 'Gone. *Basta. Finito.*'

'Gone?' I asked.

'Yeah, she left me. A lot of women aren't like you, Annie. A lot of women don't stick by their man through thick and thin.'

'I'm sorry to hear it,' I said. Now it was my turn to commiserate with his loss, and I was just as awkward as he had been over Roger's death. What else could I say?

Vanessa, I recollected, had been a rangy, laughing woman who seemed hugely proud to be Mrs Alexander O'Hara when I met her. Roger and I had been to dinner with them on at least one occasion.

'And your children?' There had been two baby boys.

He waved the hand again. 'Gone. Gone.'

'Gone where, exactly?' I queried. He must know where his children were.

'They're living in Paris. She went off with some fancy man – some bloody frog she got involved with. I think they may even be getting married. There's respectability for you! And *he* wants to adopt my sons!'

I thought this sounded most unfair. Fathers have rights too.

'She says I've been a hopeless father. But she's trying to sting me for a whole bunch of dough, claiming I haven't provided for the children.'

'And have you provided?' I was beginning to feel like an examining magistrate, though it was clearly only the usual case of casual marriage counselling, or, as is the more usual today, divorce counselling.

He nodded, though not, I thought, in a very affirmative way. 'As best I can. Things haven't gone too well in recent years. I lost the programme, as you know. Well, TV is like that – people come into fashion, people go out of fashion.'

Xan had been a highly successful television producer in the days when he was friendly with Roger. He had specialized in popular science, and had done particularly well with a programme for young people explaining science and physics. *'The World is New'* had gone out weekly when our daughter was growing up and she had loved it. It was brilliantly innovative at that time.

'What went wrong?' I asked, though I wasn't sure whether I meant the programme or the marriage: probably both.

He looked at me seriously. 'Do you know, Annie, I just can't answer that one. I just don't know the answer. But things go wrong in people's lives and there isn't a damn thing you can do about it. Look, as you're driving back to London tonight – maybe you can give me a lift?'

'Of course,' I said, hoping he was not going to repeat suggestions of seduction. I needn't have worried. Xan's taste did not run to rather drab, 47-year-old widows in the green movement. 'By the way,' I added, 'you didn't tell me what

36

you were doing here?'

'The odd article for the odd weekly magazine. Trying to turn in a shekel or two. But the expenses aren't dazzling.' As he finished his beer, I felt a stab of compassion for him. He was a man down on his luck.

I bade farewell to my ecology friends, and Xan and I left the quad at St Edmund's College in search of my Renault. One or two of the group imagined – I think – that I had casually picked up a man.

Parking is hell in Oxford, even out of term, so we had to walk to the Pay and Display Meter where I had left it, near to the Randolph Hotel. 'Let's have one for the road here,' Xan suggested, indicating the hotel's cosy bar.

I wasn't keen, but he seemed to need it. As I switched to a fruit juice, he started on another beer and a double whisky.

'I don't know what went wrong with Vanessa and me,' he took up the thread, thinking. 'But to some extent, I blame feminism. And all the ju-jitsu that you're mixed up in – ecology groups and the like. It's a substitute for human relationships.'

This stung slightly. I was committed to environmentalism, but loneliness had also propelled me towards politicization.

'Is it?' I asked sardonically. 'People who don't need some help in their relationships are very lucky, of course.'

'It's all bullshit,' he muttered. 'Women get themselves involved in all these stupid organizations which turn their heads.

'Okay, granted – I *was* travelling a lot when we were first married. But that was for the job. We had to film in the States, we filmed in the USSR, Japan, Italy. For Christ's sake, you don't turn out a top-rating TV programme every week by sitting at home in bloody Ealing!'

'Maybe Vanessa felt a little forlorn when she had to sit at home in "bloody Ealing",' I reflected. Roger had had to travel a lot too. There was always a sense of having been abandoned, of carrying the responsibilities at home while *he* sat in the Bombay Hilton discussing Third World food policies, I remembered. I could understand Vanessa's resentment of Xan's being away so often, if that indeed had been the case.

'But she was the one who always *encouraged* me to take on exciting assignments,' he said impatiently. 'She used to read the scientific mags and say – "Look what they're doing with agricultural cycles in Thailand – why don't you do a programme about it?" And I wasn't unfaithful to her. Well, not really. Abroad doesn't count.'

I had heard this theory before, from men who travelled in the course of their work. 'Abroad doesn't count.' That, of course, was all pre-AIDS.

'We went on one shoot in California,' Xan smiled, half in admiration, 'when every single member of the crew got the clap. I was the virtuous one that time. Actually I was too knackered to screw around on that project. Silicon Valley.' He thought some more and added, as an afterthought, 'Come to think of it, that whole bunch ended up divorced too.'

'Screwing around breaks up marriages,' I said simply.

'Moralizing bullshit,' said Xan.

'Not moralizing – just facts,' I shrugged.

'It's a bloody stressful life, Ann, being on the road like that. People who stay at home in comfortable London suburbs think travelling for work is fun, but it's bloody lonely and bloody stressful.'

I knew that was true. 'I know,' I said. 'You forget, Xan, that Roger was away a lot too.' Roger had been a senior agronomic adviser for the EEC.

Then Xan said a weird thing. 'In a way, I envy you Annie. When a spouse dies suddenly at the age of 42, you are left with a memory of marriage that is perfectly intact. Being widowed is so much less disillusioning than being divorced. It is so much better in every way.'

I felt so stunned by this remark that I literally could not reply. Widowhood, for me, had been such a shock – there had been such a profound sense of anger and loss – that I felt insulted and furious at Xan's words.

He just did not know what he was talking about. I sometimes felt this sense of fury and frustration against divorced people, who seemed to have thrown away what had been torn from me so cruelly – the substance of a marriage.

I stood up and so did Xan. He called good-night to the landlord, clubbably, as we departed and made for the car.

I clipped in my seat belt and pointed Xan at his. 'Don't wear seat-belts,' he said abruptly. 'Don't believe in them. Those who love their life too dearly shall lose it. Those who are careless of their lives shall guard them.' It was some tipsy interpretation of a Biblical quote.

'If you should smash your brains on my windscreen,' I said, exerting control. 'I'd like you to know it is not my responsibility.'

'Okey-dokey,' he rejoined.

We started off and I had to concentrate for a while. Getting out of Oxford is almost as difficult as parking within it – it is full of ill-signposted, one-way streets. This is Oxford's way of stating its superiority to the mere visitor. Despite his intox-ication, Xan proved a reliable navigator, and we were soon over the Cherwell and on the Cowley Road.

'I'm sorry if I offended you back there,' Xan mumbled. 'I shouldn't patronize you by telling you that widowhood is wonderful. I'm bloody sure it isn't.'

I was glad Xan wasn't so thick-skinned that he hadn't noticed my ire.

'You can say that again,' I said flatly.

'But I'll tell you this, Ann. We did a programme on marriage – it was more sociology than science – but it revealed one important truth to me. The average Victorian marriage was happy and stable because it lasted, on average, ten to fifteen years. Marriages were happy because people died. Most people can be happy for ten to fifteen years. The intervention of death saves marriages.'

I could have taken up the monkey-wrench I kept in the glove compartment of the car and brained him there and then, if we hadn't been moving onto the dual carriageway at Headington.

'I'm sure your marriage to Roger was idyllic – idyllic,' he stressed. 'I'm just saying that losing him in his prime, like that, leaves you with all the good memories, without the disappointments that set in later.'

I felt near to tears, inside. I had that urge – which had been diminishing in the last couple of years – to tell Roger about this. I wanted to laugh with him over the sheer lumpen idiocy of Xan O'Hara.

'Oh, I know I'm being a shit,' Xan said then, taking a small flask of whisky from his inside pocket. I'm just bloody embittered. When I think how happy Vanessa and I were, to begin with. We were like that.' He held up two fingers, intertwined. 'Like that! No secrets from one another. Marriage of true minds. And bodies. Our sex life was stupendous. Every night, sometimes every morning too. And she gave up her job. She didn't want to teach maths any more, she said. She just wanted to be *my wife*.' He shook his head at the wonder of it.

'She occasionally came with me on a foreign trip, but she was more inclined to stay at home, especially when the boys were born. Vanessa was *domesticated*. She loved doing up the house and she was the most dedicated mother. Not to speak of the animals she cared for! The dog, the cat, the hamster, the gerbil, the bloody goldfish. We didn't entertain a lot because our lives were wrapped up with one another.

'Okay, I can see now I became highly embroiled in my work. Highly embroiled.' He had the drunk's habit of emphasis through repetition. 'But that was the way things went. She was ambitious for me, for Christ's sake. She wanted me to do well. And it brought in a lot of money at the time, which she wholly appreciated. Vanessa likes the best, you know. I brought her some Estée Lauder fragrance once from a short trip to Amsterdam, and she turned up her nose at it. Only *French* perfume. 'Course, after that, I always brought her *French* perfume. But you know what television is – you earn a lot, you spend a lot.'

We were nearing the motorway now, and it was starting to rain. Night was down.

'You can smoke if you want to,' I told him, though I hated it in the car. Despite myself, I was getting sorry for Xan again.

'So bloody tolerant, Ann,' he smiled. 'Actually, I'd like a pee, first.'

Obediently, I drew into a lay-by and he got out to relieve himself. Why the dickens didn't he think of this before he left the hotel, I thought. Xan was not a planner.

He returned like a drenched mongrel, his hair curled by the rain.

'That was just what the children used to do,' he said nostalgically.

He took out the permitted cigarette. 'It was when the children started to go to school – that was when Vanessa began to get restless. We were eleven or twelve years married at the time, and the kids were at this bloody good, but bloody expensive, school which worked their little butts off. Vanessa was more at a loose end than she'd imagined she would be. She suddenly said she'd like to take a Russian course, of all things. I couldn't particularly see the sense of this.

'I mean, I didn't see any harm in it either. Vanessa's speciality had been maths – why suddenly take up learning Russian at the age of thirty-six? But she said she wanted to do something new, creative. We had a very capable Swedish *au pair* at the time. Blonde. Big tits. It gave Vanessa the chance to pursue her creativity, as she put it.' He delivered this in a funny-genteel Edinburgh accent, signalling that he thought extra-mural classes for housewives a high affectation.

'Well, the recession began to hit in the mid-70s, and the independent TV companies started to rein in their resources a bit. Still, the ratings were okay, and there was plenty to do. It's true, I was drinking more than usual – but I'd never exactly been a teetotaller.

'Vanessa started to get deeply *involved* with this group of

Jewish women at the Russian classes. The Campaign for fucking Refuseniks. Pardon my French. They were learning Russian to communicate with Jews in the USSR. Okay. A nice little hobby for rich and bored Hampstead ladies. Better than having an affair with their psychiatrist.'

'Xan!' I ticked him off. 'Campaigning for dissidents has been wonderfully altruistic work – and it's paid off!'

'Okay, okay.' He took another slug of his whisky. 'That's great. It just happens that just at the moment Vanessa was getting a high profile with a dedicated Jewish lobby, I'm doing a deal with the Saudis to supply them with a series of films on the development of medicine. It just happens I'm doing a special assignment to Moscow to report on eye surgery there. Brezhnev's Moscow, remember? The question is, Annie, was she doing all this to fulfill her altruistic side, or, somehow to fuck me up?'

'Pardon your French,' I added.

'Yeah. And then these political rows would start. I couldn't understand it. Vanessa never had had that much interest in politics before. She was always some kind of wishy-washy liberal, but nothing very definite. But one thing led to another, and she began to get mixed up with all kinds of people. I mean, the rich Jewish ladies were harmless enough, but that soon led on to women's groups who were pretty damn *subversive*.'

He looked out at the drizzle. He presented a mournful face to the world. There was a harmonious silence until we passed the exit for Slough. 'Come friendly bombs, and rain on Slough,' he sighed.

'There isn't grass to graze a cow,' I went on. 'Rain over, death!'

'When did you actually split up?' I prompted him.

'We had a lot of fights, then. I asked her not to make herself conspicuous on these anti-Soviet demos; then she gets her picture in the *Evening Standard* waving a banner outside the Russian Embassy in Kensington. "TV Man's Wife in Refusenik

Demo." And surprise, surprise,' he shook his head, his mouth set in a sour grimace, 'I don't get my working visa for the Soviet Union. And so the big programme on eye surgery is aborted. God, I screamed at her after that. She said I had no principles. She called me "a mere careerist". Our sex life was at zero. I consoled myself, I admit it. I didn't get married to live like a monk. Though I'm damn near living like a monk today.'

'You get accustomed to celibacy,' I told him calmly.

He looked at me in horror. 'Dammit, I'm only forty-seven.'

'So am I.'

He said nothing, but Xan was a male chauvinist born and bred, and I knew he was thinking 'It's different for women.' I am not entirely sure I don't agree with him, though I would never admit that in so many words.

We had passed the M25 and were heading towards London now.

'Where are you living, Xan?' I asked.

'In a small, over-priced dump between Kings Cross and Islington.'

'And your lovely double-fronted Victorian home?'

'Sold. Proceeds divided. I invested mine in a new company that went bust – thanks to the bloody unions in the film business. She invested hers in a flat in Paris, where she's living with this Jewish guy she's teamed up with. They're full time into international refugee stuff now. She's big on the Afghans. Her anti-Soviet form has helped her there.'

'And your sons?'

'Casimir is in school here in England. I see him one or twice a term. But don't worry – I get all the bills. Ernest is at a day-school in France. He'll grow up a Frenchman.'

From what Xan had said, it seemed to me that Vanessa had indeed been somewhat unreasonable. Why hadn't she talked to him more about what she wanted, instead of rushing off and damaging his career? How could she have changed from the good-tempered woman I had met to a quarrelsome political activist?

'I'd give a lot to be on civil terms with Vanessa again,' Xan said, as we travelled through the limbo of those outer London suburbs: Ickenham, Harefield, Hillingdon, Northolt, Ruislip, Southall, driving towards the Great Western Avenue in a night now clear and almost free of traffic. 'When I think of the scrubbers I've been with . . . dismal dames without background, without culture. We had such a great marriage in the early days. It was unforgettable.

'My career will pick up again,' he said, more optimistically. 'Nuclear power will come back into fashion. They'll forget Chernobyl.' Then I remembered what I'd heard about Xan's track record. He had been a staunch defender of nuclear energy all along; but just three days before the disaster at Chernobyl, he had published a long article in one of the specialist weeklies claiming that the Russians were coping particularly well with the management of their nuclear industry. It had been bad luck for Xan's reputation.

As we approached West London, I offered to drive him over to Kings Cross. He shook his head. 'Wouldn't hear of it. It's only ten thirty, and it's bloody decent of you to let me come along with you.' He looked at me with amiability. 'And it's helped me to talk about all this. The pubs are still open, however, so you can drop me anywhere around here and I'll have a nightcap. Where are you living, by the way?'

'Bloody Acton,' I told him. 'Not far from Bloody Ealing.'

'*Touché*!' he grinned. 'You must give me your number, Annie. I'll phone you some time and we'll murder a few drams when you're not driving.'

'I'm in the book,' I told him. I was still listed under Roger's name, too. He couldn't miss it.

I left Xan off, at his own request, near Park Royal tube station – not far from where they make Guinness, appropriately. I went home, then, to a starving cat. I had only decided to drive back to London that night for the cat's sake. We all need something to care for.

It is a small world, as people have been known to observe;

44

small, really, because people who share the same interests often go to the same places. Opera-lovers constantly run into one another at Covent Garden, and regular swimmers find like-minded souls at Chelsea swimming baths. So it was not extraordinarily strange that I saw Vanessa O'Hara three weeks later at a vegetarian restaurant off Tottenham Court Road.

I am a vegetarian, so it was natural for me to eat there. But it is also the sort of place which tends to be patronized by pottery-throwing feminists. I spotted Vanessa with a group of other women in a corner when I was standing in line to pay for my lunch. As I ate, I glanced at her occasionally. She was chatting away animatedly. She had changed remarkably little – except that her hair was shorter. Her laughing good temper seemed unaltered by the crabby politicization that Xan had implied.

Her companions left ahead of her – she remained to drink more coffee. It was curiosity as much as courtesy which propelled me over to her table.

'Vanessa,' I said. 'I'm Ann Bellinger. Roger Bellinger's . . . wife.' I always introduce myself, as I don't expect people to remember me. I have the sort of mousey face, anyway, that I am sure is instantly forgettable.

She looked up at me, uncertain for a moment, searching the computer of her mind for the relevant data that would bring recognition. Then it flashed up on the inner screen. She smiled sunnily. 'Yes, Ann. I remember. How *are* you?' Then she stopped in her tracks. 'I was sorry to read of Roger's death. I saw the obituary. I did mean to write to you at the time, but we were just off to Pakistan and . . .'

'Thank you,' I said, although I would indeed have preferred a letter of condolence at the time. 'May I join you?' I sat. 'I'm fine, thanks. It's nearly five years now, and I've managed quite well. Our daughter is grown up and at Durham University, where she's very happy – I seldom see her, indeed. She's off to Austria during the vacation.'

'Well done,' said Vanessa. 'You're a free woman – now you've your daughter off your hands.'

'Yes,' I said, although I didn't necessarily think of Candida as being 'off my hands'; or perhaps I didn't want to.

'Some of Roger's interests have rubbed off on me – I've become very involved in the ecology movement. All those studies on fertilization of crops that I typed – they came in handy!'

'So you're working now?' she said. 'Your husband used to consider it a matter of pride that you stayed at home – just as mine did,' Vanessa said. 'Of course, you know that Alexander and I split up? I'm living in Paris now – I'm only over in London to do a Channel Four programme about women refugees.' So that explained the ladies in boiler suits with whom she had lunched: Channel Four executives.

'Yes,' I said, eager to unburden my conscience now. 'Actually, you will think this extraordinary, but I drove your husband from Oxford just a few weeks ago. I saw him at a conference on nuclear energy – one given by our side, actually – and he said he'd appreciate a lift back to London.'

'Yes,' said Vanessa drily. 'He'd like that. Something for nothing. How did he seem?'

I told her non-commitally that Xan seemed fine.

'Drinking?'

'A little.'

Her nostrils flared. Flaring nostrils are wonderfully attractive, I thought. They look so noble and disdainful. 'You mean a lot, don't you? You don't have to shield Xan's habits from me. I lived with him for fifteen miserable years.'

'He spoke about that,' I said to her. 'He spoke with much regret that the marriage had dissolved.'

'He has a great deal to regret,' she said primly. 'You know, Ann, in some ways – look, I know it's a ghastly thing to say, but it's still true – you're lucky to be a widow. At least you have a good memory of your marriage. At least it isn't poisoned by the rat trying to jeopardize custodial care of the children.'

How do they know, I asked myself, that a widow only has good memories, all these divorced people who tell me that I'm so 'lucky'? It's the bad memories, the times you didn't do your best, that put the icy hoar on widowhood.

'How are your sons?' I asked, not wishing to comment – not trusting myself – on my 'luck' at being a widow, though God knows I still hate that word. I had started life as a sub-editor on a small newspaper in Cambridge, when we called a left-over word on a line, a word to be dropped from the passage, a 'widow'.

'They're fine,' Vanessa said brightly. 'They are so much happier now that I am more serene. It's frightful for children when parents quarrel. And they get on so well with David, the man I share my life with now.' It sounded so – egalitarian and democratic: the man I share my life with. 'Xan was such a hopeless father. He never took any interest in the children. He never took any real interest in me either. He wasn't concerned with what I was thinking – he just complacently wanted me as his wife.'

I reminded her that they seemed to get on terrifically well on the occasions Roger and I had seen them together.

'Yes, well, that was the early years,' she said dismissively. Suddenly she interjected, 'Would you like a coffee?', which was thoughtful. But I never drink more than one cup of coffee a day, so I declined.

'People generally get on well during the early years of marriage,' Vanessa went on. 'And Xan was different then. He was a bright young man, so enthusiastic, with all these innovatory ideas. He was so responsive to ideas. When I'd say "Why don't you do a programme about DNA – really explain it" – he'd say "What a fabulous idea" and just go off and do it. He was optimistic and energetic. Our sex life was wonderful at the beginning. He was so considerate, so generous in bed. He seemed to be generous financially in those days, too. I was absorbed in the house and with his work, too, and with having babies, and I didn't much want to do anything else.'

'Yes, I understand,' I said.

'The trouble was that Xan began to take it all for granted,' she said, her long fingers playing with the plant which adorned the wooden table. 'He began to think that all this terminal domesticity would be the whole of my life. Whereas it was only a phase of my life. Women like to be enclosed when they are at the baby-making phase, but that doesn't last forever. Nor should it. For example, he never wanted to bring anyone home. You came over once, I remember, but it was rarely that we entertained. Xan didn't like his home invaded by other people. On the other hand, he was away a lot of the time, and that didn't help either. When he was abroad I didn't want to entertain, because it's no fun on your own.'

'I've discovered that,' I said.

'It seems strange I should be telling you this so precipitately,' Vanessa said. 'But I'm sure you got his version, and I think you should hear mine.'

Divorced partners often feel that if the opposition has nobbled a witness, their side should have a hearing too.

'Then he became so wildly unreasonable when I said I wanted to take up Russian. Honestly, you'd think I'd applied to join the IRA. One day, when I was complaining about the cost of London schools, he actually said to me: "I don't know why you don't keep the children at home and educate them yourself. There's a growing home-education movement." I would have been nicely boxed in, for his liking, wouldn't I? A thoroughly domesticated wife and mother imprisoned in her own home!

'Of course, men always punish women when women slip out of their control. One evening the Russian class was cancelled because the teacher had flu, and I came home early . . . to find him having sex with the Swedish au pair. *In flagrante*! In our bedroom!

'I'm not a jealous wife,' Vanessa stressed. 'I don't make scenes if a man flirts with other women. And I know indiscretions go on during foreign trips: "abroad doesn't count", and all that. But at home? Hammer and tongs in one's own bedroom, while the children were playing with the Scalectrix upstairs? No!'

Vanessa had lowered her voice during this passage. Vegetarians always look so proper, don't they? I suppose I am proper, because I was shocked: shocked, too, that he had left this vital element out of his evidence.

'Obviously this created a rift,' she concluded. 'And then he was drinking far too much – no wonder his career was going downhill. And then I did get involved with some wonderful women at the Russian class who were campaigning for Soviet refuseniks. The stories of the refuseniks were just heart-breaking – such brave, brave people. And of course he cut up rough about that. Said I was ruining his relationship with the Russians. But why didn't *he* do something to help the dissidents in Russia? He was in a very good position to try and influence things. But he wouldn't touch it.'

Vanessa ran her fingers through her short tousled hair, and her green eyes were still full of anger and a curiously passionate hatred. 'I mean, when you measure the persecution of victims of totalitarianism against anything we endure . . . there is no contest, is there? We helped to bring about *glasnost*, after all. Xan has been wrong-footed by sticking to all those dullards from the Brezhnev era. I'm proud of what we did – we got scores of Jews out of the USSR and improved the atmosphere for other dissidents too.'

I could see that Vanessa had found a cause that had animated her, and a different sort of husband might have been more supportive to her. But a different sort of wife might have campaigned less publicly, or taken care not to let her activities damage a husband's career.

'Oh, it all went to pieces,' she looked sadly at the dregs of the coffee. 'He was very promiscuous. He never took enough interest in the children – Casimir developed a frightening ear infection and it was all left to me. He was very concerned about work at this stage, I know. God knows I had to listen to him complaining, night after night, about his enemies and his funding difficulties and all the rest of it. He wouldn't be told that he was drinking too much.'

'It's a stressful life, TV,' I said, in some spirit of defence.

'Stress, schmess,' she responded in mock-Yiddish. 'Mining is stressful, being a charwoman is stressful, being a waitress is stressful, being a teacher is stressful. But they don't put on airs and graces about it: they don't think it gives them permission to screw around or to have vodka for breakfast. TV executives should try to be refugees for a while. Then they'd know about stress!'

'Xan mentioned you worked with refugees now,' I said.

'He seems to have given you chapter and verse indeed,' she raised an eyebrow. 'Yes, I do – David –' she pronounced it the French way, Daa-veed – 'David and I do that together. I feel I am now making a real contribution to humanity. I'm not just somebody's wife any more, holed up in Ealing. I'm a real person in my own right.'

She was pleased with how she had emerged from the *débâcle* of the end of the marriage. Still, I reflected waspishly, relationships, like marriages, always go well at the beginning. See if Daaveed lasts fifteen years.

'Of course, I'd like to have a cordial relationship with Xan,' she mused. 'But on the last two occasions that I tried, he was just so completely drunk and abusive that it was impossible. He turned up at Casimir's school paralytic. And he constantly reneges on the boys' education and maintenance fees. It's just fortunate that David is magnanimous towards them.'

She said nothing about re-marrying, or about Daaveed adopting the boys. I wondered if the idea was Xan's paranoia. Indeed, she indicated to the contrary. 'Marriage is for children, don't you think?' she said. 'Once you've had your children, what's the point?'

I could have mentioned several, such as the romantic, idealistic, marriage vows about cleaving together as long as you both shall live; I could have conjured up the fancy of a Darby and Joan, growing old in sweet companionship, inseparable.

Vanessa looked at her watch. 'I must fly,' she said. 'Let me give you my card – in case you're ever in Paris.' She extracted an elegant Franch visiting card from a wallet. I thanked her. I told her I didn't carry a card, but my address and number were in the telephone book, still under Roger's name.

We parted cordially – she on her way to Channel Four in

Charlotte Street, I to Heals, to change some blinds for my daughter's bedroom.

How fragile is modern marriage, I reflected, as I crossed Tottenham Court Road. It could so quickly deteriorate from a gossamer idyll into a squalid fight, in which each side only told, and only saw, *their* side of the story. If only people could . . . grit their teeth a little perhaps, and weather these storms. Vanessa might have saved Xan from descending into a drunken depression; he could have helped her towards some personal fulfilment within the marriage.

Still, I told myself, I mustn't preach. It seldom achieves anything. And really, how could I be sure that my own marriage would have endured? We had just celebrated our fifteenth anniversary when Roger died. That was the allotted span of the happy Victorian union, if Xan were right. That's what they both meant by saying I was 'lucky'; and in a way, perhaps I was. I had certainly never been disillusioned about my husband.

'Abroad doesn't count', they had both said. I didn't like that phrase. I really didn't like it one little bit.

The European Spirit

I sometimes wondered if Helena Green aspired to celebrate our entry into the Common Market by acquiring a lover from each of the member countries. This was in 1973, so there were only nine states in the EEC at the time – lucky Norway, missed being notched up by a referendum's whisker! (I suppose she made Switzerland an honorary member during a ski-ing holiday! Many times over, if I knew Helena!)

She called all this man-catching 'showing the European Spirit', or being *'communitaire'*. This was one of the great catch-cries among the EEC folk at Brussels at the time – *'communitaire'*. It means having the European spirit. If sleeping around was *'communitaire'*, Helena had a positive mission for it.

I sound catty, don't I? I sound as though I didn't like Helena. But I did. Enormously. She was a funny, warm, vibrant girl with an angelic face and blonde hair – well, coloured blonde anyway – who attracted men as naturally as trees draw song birds on a spring morning. It wasn't just because of her looks. It was because she breathed this air of freedom. She would stride around with a loose shoulder-bag swinging from her any-old-how, making other women seem somehow prim and guarded. If I am a bit *sharp* about Helena, possibly it's because I was a bit of a plain mouse in contrast, who felt grateful if any man took the slightest interest in me. I always felt anxious about meeting men, hoping for a nice, safe one. I was the prudent one.

I was the sort of young woman who always took her Dutch cap to a party even if nothing remotely romantic was likely to happen; and generally I ended up going home alone to the sweet little flat Helena and I shared in the Square Marguerite.

Helena was the one who frequently didn't come home. And who frequently forgot her Dutch cap even in the most auspicious circs. That is, when she bothered owning one at all.

We were an unlikely pair when it came to flat-sharing, not only because of our different personalities, but also because of our different status. The Common Market bureaucracy, like all bureaucracies, is very status-conscious. I was a secretary at the Commission – that's the bureaucracy which runs the European Community – while Helena was an interpreter. We had both come to Brussels in the early 1970s, in preparation really for the European Community expansion which would include Britain, Ireland and Denmark in '73. We had known each other at Trinity College Dublin, where we had both done modern languages. But I'd never have had the nerve to be an interpreter. It's very interesting but very stressful work and you have to have a streak of the performer and the public speaker in you – you've got to translate jokes while thinking on your feet, and you mustn't hit the wrong note or make an error. I'm a desk sort of person, whereas Helena could easily have gone on the stage. Not a nervous streak in her body. But we basically got on, and we ended up sharing this flat, (and a cat called Bijou).

Although we worked in the same building – the famous Berlaymont, which, I assure you, could be the setting for a Euro-soap opera any day of the week – we didn't see much of each other at work. Then again, Helena travelled overseas quite a bit. She did both French and Italian into English – the general rule is that you interpret into your mother tongue – and was needed for overseas aid conferences in North Africa – Tunisia, Morocco, Algiers – and in Ethiopia and Libya where, for historical reasons, the managing *élite* speaks Italian. She also trucked up and down to Luxembourg and Strasbourg on European Community business.

There was ample opportunity for the *'communitaire'* encounters that Helena favoured. And there were, I recall, some very nice guys in her life.

There was a merry German called Wolfgang Peters – married, of course, but mad about Helena. He was fat and sexy. Afterwards he divorced his wife: alas, by then Helena was out of all our lives, otherwise I'm sure he'd have wanted to marry her.

There was a Dutchman, Piet. He was a bit earnest, lanky and left-wing, but he had a wry side which could be amusing. Helena liked to laugh. I remember now that he was obsessed with stuff about pollution and ecology. Then there was a generous Dane who took us both for enormous meals in the Boulevard Anspach. There was also a very grand French civil servant who showered her with gifts from Givenchy and Saint-Laurent.

'Tell me, Hells,' I asked her – I sometimes called her Hells Bells, or Hells – over breakfast one morning after another night on the town. 'What exactly have you got against the Italians?'

'Oh Blakey,' she retorted – my name then was Briony Blake – 'don't be daft. Italians are adorable. "Carissima, Bellissima". But,' she went on eating ice-cream, her eccentric breakfast food chosen on the theory that it lined your stomach after drinking, 'you have to be prudent with Italians just the same.'

'What a sensible word to hear from your lips, Helena dear,' I said, with a light, affectionate sarcasm. *'Prudent.* Very nice indeed.'

'Well, I am in my way. There's method in the madness, don't you know. I haven't had an Italian boyfriend – well, not lately anyhow – because . . . no suitable candidate has been offered. But you do have to be more careful with Mediterranean men. They still tend to think of women as either madonnas or whores. They don't understand Women's Liberation. Italians think that if you jump into bed with them you're some kind of little tart. They don't understand it's just a free choice you're making. You should talk to your sewing-circle ladies about it. They would tell you this is well-established old wives' wisdom.'

Helena made fun of my needlework group, which met every second Tuesday evening in the pretty suburb of Ixelles. I had begun to be friendly with a shy Englishman called Keith who rather diligently went to a Flemish class on Tuesday nights, and I would go off to sew while he went off to learn throaty Dutch verbs. Helena thought needlework stuffy beyond measure, but I liked it, belonging to a group had helped me broaden my friendships, and we did lots of projects for charity, which made me feel, somehow, worthwhile. I had been introduced to this craft project by Philippa Shields, another friend from Dublin University days, who was now married to one of the top Irish Eurocrats at the Commission.

Basically, Helena was tolerant of my cosy hobby, just as I was quite open-minded about her hectic life. In a funny way, we complemented each other extraordinarily well. You see, I think that for all Helena's extrovert brains and high-velocity living, she needed a bit of stability and continuity in her life; she certainly needed someone who would remember to pay the telephone bill. While I enjoyed, vicariously, watching Helena take risks which would just not have been in my personality, even if I'd had the looks.

I knew that it was part of Helena's character to take risks, but I still puzzled over her extraordinary lack of care when it came to contraception. She was the one who talked about Women's Liberation, and how women were truly free for the first time in history because of the Pill. And yet, she wouldn't take the Pill herself – claiming it sent up her blood pressure. Neither would she resort to any other known method. She dismissed my reliable old Dutch cap as 'unromantic'; and in those pre-AIDS days, the condom was considered crude. 'National Service issue,' Helena called French letters, referring to the fact that men doing military service in the UN were issued with them. (Helena had done an entire interpretation spell about this once, noting that the French for 'French letter' was *capote Anglaise* –

English hood.) There had been, apparently, much discussion over the usefulness of *capotes Anglaises* as a prophylactic against venereal disease among prostitutes. Helena didn't like the connection of condoms with whores, but I suspect she also didn't like the fact that they were a sensible precaution which worked. She was funny that way. I think now she hadn't at all worked out her basic attitudes to sexuality and fertility, for all her confident talk about feminism and choice.

What she used for contraception was a sort of vague fertility-cycle method which she had devised herself, with the assistance of – wait for it! – a Roman Catholic manual on the Rhythm Method! Helena was not a Roman Catholic; in fact, her folks had been minor Irish Protestant gentry who, judging from the mores of Trinity College Dublin of our day, rather despised Roman Catholicism as a sort of peasant superstition. But this Rhythm Method sort of appealed to Helena. I believe it was colloquially known as 'Vatican roulette' and, you see, she had a sort of Russian roulette personality. It was the risk-taking element that she found *exciting*. It was the hit and miss that turned her on.

And there were misses. 'A trip to London is on the cards,' she would announce. She knew she was pregnant, she always said, when champagne started to taste metallic.

'Oh, you silly cow, Helena,' I'd grimace. 'How could you be such a damn fool!' Abortion was illegal in Belgium at the time – still is, theoretically – so women had to go to London to get rid of a pregnancy.

It wasn't that I had any moral objections – I certainly didn't, and I still don't. I think abortion should be available, within reason, to any woman who wants it. But repeated abortion is just silly. It can't be good for your health, and it is a sign that a woman isn't taking care of herself. And it does take its toll, in a way. A woman loses something.

Of course, Helena always put on a brave, indeed a defiant face, on it. She combined the 'TOP', as she called it (termination of pregnancy – the clinical term she has had occasion to see on her medical papers at least five times), with a shopping trip. She always returned with a different hairstyle, as though she wanted to change herself again. But even Helena couldn't shake off that slight air of wistfulness that can follow an abortion. She always made an immense, maternal fuss of the cat afterwards.

Helena never involved the men in her 'TOPs'. She regarded it as her responsibility, her decision. She was strong that way. She faced the consequences of her action.

Time passed and my English boyfriend grew fonder. He was really very nice. We spent a weekend together in Antwerp. He was astonishingly ardent. It was divine. I began to feel much less of a mouse.

Philippa Shields also went to London a couple of times that year. She told me about her problem in the car driving back from our Ixelles sewing circle. She was seeing a fertility specialist in London, she said. She and Mike were childless and she was desperate to have a baby.

I thought it was so ironic that Helena should have to go to London to abort a baby while Philippa was making the same trip in order to get one. Typical of life!

Presently, in the autumn of 1974, Helena finally succumbed to an Italian! They had met on European Community business in Copenhagen. And this time, it struck me, the relationship really meant something to Helena.

Claudio seemed an untypical Italian, I thought at the time; reserved, tall, bespectacled, sandy-haired. He was drawn to Helena because of her vivacity, I think. During their short romance, Helena was at her most elated, enraptured, energetic. She laughed a great deal, I remember, in those months. Of course Claudio was married, but what the hell? His wife was in Milan. It didn't matter. They were happy.

Then the inevitable happened. The champagne started to go metallic. As usual, she told me over breakfast. This time she was distinctly less ebullient.

'It's bloody London again, Blakey,' she said gloomily.

I was feeding the cat.

'I am not sorry for you this time, Helena,' I said, with real severity.

It struck me then, probably consciously for the first time, that the joke was wearing a bit thin. I was maturing. My own relationship with Keith had focused my mind – and my heart – more on love and commitment, and I was beginning to be less amused by Helena's raffishness. She was funny and she was fun, but she was also irresponsible.

'You should know better by now, Helena,' I told her off. 'You're twenty-six and you're abusing your body with these abortions.'

'It is *my body*,' she replied sulkily. 'I can do what I like with it.'

'Yes, well maybe one day you'll *want* a baby,' I said. 'And then maybe you'll find, like poor Phillipa Shields, that you can't *have* one. Did you ever think about that?'

Helena shook her head. 'I'll never want a baby,' she said, with a forlorn kind of certainty. 'I'm sure of that. I'm not fit to be a mother. For Christ's sake, Briony!' She took out a cigarette, although she rarely smoked.

'You can't be sure,' I said. Was I trying to comfort her or to discipline her? 'People change their minds. When you meet the right man . . .'

'I've met the right man,' Helena said. 'Claudio is the right man. But he's never going to leave his wife. It's been explained to me from zero. His wife is a textile millionairess. In Milan. She's funded his political career. They have three children. He is the man of my life, but I wouldn't ask him to make that sacrifice for me. I do have some honour, you know. I might be a man-catcher, but I don't inveigle husbands away from their wives, careers, property, families.'

I tried a different tack.

'Of course,' I said. 'You could always have the baby, as a single mother. It's becoming more acceptable now, you know.'

It's funny, isn't it? I said I wasn't moralistic about abortion, and I'm not. But I still felt that five was too many. It's always a matter, isn't it, of unfinished business? For some reason, this time, I felt Helena should go through with the pregnancy. She had always taken the consequences of her actions; maybe I felt this was the ultimate consequence; maybe I felt that this would, at last, settle her down.

In some way, Helena felt that too. I had never seen her so gloomy about the prospect of a TOP.

Then she said suddenly: 'I've got an idea. Why don't I have the baby, and *give* it to Phillipa Shields? That would solve everyone's problem!'

I thought she was joking, of course. 'That's rot,' I said, just in case she wasn't joking. 'You can't just give babies to people. There is a bureaucracy in charge of such matters. Just like the Common Market! They're called social workers! *They* organize adoptions, nowadays!'

Philippa had actually talked to me about this. Although they had wanted a baby of their very own, they had looked at the adoption situation. It was full of red tape.

Helena gave me a smile: a very naughty smile, too. 'Anyway.' she said, 'you could say I owe it to Philippa. There was a brief episode with Mike.'

'Well!' I said, mock exasperated. 'I'm glad Ireland got a piece of the action, with your so-called "European spirit"! If only for old times sake!'

We did laugh, though. I could have murdered her, but we laughed just the same.

The next few months were very busy. We had a big programme on regional policy and a big pow-wow on transport policy, and I didn't see a lot of Helena. She was travelling a great deal. She went to London and I assumed that she'd had her TOP, though she indicated that she didn't want to talk about it, and there was no change of hairstyle. I think she was still seeing Claudio. But there was more overseas work too, including a trip to the Sahel region of Western Africa. She returned from there shattered, drained.

60

'The poverty,' she shook her head, woebegone. 'The starvation. The children in need. It's pitiful.' She was paler, softer and more serious that I had ever seen her.

'Too many children in the world,' I replied tartly. And pointedly I added: 'Better family planning policies would save a lot of suffering.'

'Human nature isn't like that, Briony,' Helena said, thoughtfully. 'The poorer people are, the more they *need* to have children. The more their children die, the more they need to compensate by having more children. The world just isn't filled with nice, middle-class people who can remember to take the Pill as they brush their teeth.'

In a way, perhaps Helena identified with all those poor people who were chaotic about family planning, I thought. Without having the excuse of famine and disaster, she had the same mentality.

'Did you ever talk to Philippa Shields about my idea?' Helena then asked.

'About babies? Well . . .' I went on, 'I didn't think there was much point.'

Helena was unpacking, sitting on the floor. She had taken to wearing weird African clothes which was consonant with some of the late-hippy fashions of the time.

'I didn't have the TOP,' she said, by way of explanation. 'By the time I got to the clinic in Regents Park, I thought, what the hell. It's too boring to go through the routine again. It's time I did something positive, *je me suis dit*.'

I knelt down next to her. 'Dear Helena,' I said softly. 'Are you all right?'

'Yes,' she said. 'I'm fine.' She was playing with an ill-made little African necklace.

'Have you told Claudio?'

She shook her head. 'No. It's too complicated.'

'What are you going to do?'

'I'm going to have the baby,' she said looking up at me with a kind of triumph. 'I'm over five months pregnant. Under all this,' she indicated her roomy kaftan, 'it's *just* beginning to show. And,' she added, 'I'm going to give the baby up for adoption. So it might as well be Philippa who does the adopting.'

'You might change your mind,' I told her, again. 'People do.'

'I know people do, but I won't,' she looked sideways, the whites of her eyes showing. 'I know I won't. Now I want you to be sensible and arrange it, Blakey. You know what to do. You're the level-headed one.'

Well, I got in touch with Philippa Shields, ringing her up with a silly pretext about a knitting pattern that involved a travelling vine motif. I said I had to show her the work. We arranged to have coffee one day in the Avenue Louise.

We met and had the coffee, and I had to call for a brandy before I embarked on the business of telling her about Helena's plans. I was *very* awkward. I muttered away about Helena's pregnancy, and how she was interested in finding adopters.

Phillipa looked dubious, as well she might. She had met Helena, briefly, and didn't particularly like her. Helena was not the kind of woman that wives like.

In the end, I explained that I would be away for much of the summer – I had some extended leave coming up – but that Helena would be at the flat, and if Philippa wanted to take the idea any further, well, she could ring and talk.

Philippa then mortified me by asking me about the knitting pattern that troubled me. Of course, in all my nervousness, I'd forgotten to bring it along!

I was going to be away for the summer – back in the old UK, a summer that began particularly early for me that year. Keith and I were going to get married. We were going to meet in London, and then visit my mother in Wales, and then spend a while in the Lake District, near his parents in Kendal. I'd had my leave saved up – the European Community was generous about holidays anyway – and there was an American girl coming to stay in the flat at Square Marguerite. She was doing a thesis on bi-lingual conflicts and Belgium was a useful base. She promised to look after Bijou, too.

Helena and I had a wistful evening meal together before I departed. The pregnancy was showing, but she was continuing to work. She had boldly announced the fact of the pregnancy to her boss, who took it calmly. She never really made it clear what Claudio's reaction had been. He seemed to be spending a lot of time that year back in Italy. Life is cushy for European Community executives, and he had been able to arrange things to his convenience, too, it seemed.

'Here's looking at you, kid,' I told her, half-mockingly, as we shared a bottle of particularly good champagne which, now, she could hardly taste.

'We've had fun, Blakey,' was all she said. 'We've had great fun.'

I told her that I would be back in Brussels in September, and I expected to find a bottle of The Widow – *la Veuve Cliquot* champagne – in the fridge when I returned, and when she'd be able to taste it again.

'It'll be there,' she said.

Keith and I had a blissful summer in England and Wales. My mother doted on him immediately. I found his parents shy, like him, but sweet. We saw a gypsy horse fair in Westmoreland, and in London, we walked by the river and kissed like teenagers. We made our happy plans. I would return to Brussels in the autumn and we would marry, we hoped, in the spring. Keith worked for a property consultancy in Belgium, but was more interested, really, in folklore than in real estate; he was hoping to get a job with the British Council, and if he did, we would go wherever his work took him.

When I got back to Brussels in September I found the American girl, Kathy, alone with our cat. Everything seemed in order, but Helena had disappeared. She had arranged things very properly. She had paid her share of the rent until Christmas, and packed up all of her things.

A bottle of Veuve Cliquot champagne stood in the fridge. 'Enjoy it, Blakey,' she had written on the bottle. 'And think of me.'

I made enquiries among the Brussels interpreters, and discovered very little, except that Helena had quit her job. Further investigation on the grapevine revealed the curious fact that Philippa Shields, and her husband, had disappeared to Ireland. And, surprise, surprise, Claudio was in Washington, representing the European Community there.

It was a strange time. I wrote to the old address that I had had for Helena in Ireland – her parents were not living, but she kept a base in County Kildare there with an elderly aunt – but received no response.

Well: life in Brussels – as elsewhere – never stands still. There are always lots of changes going on. There is a rotating principle in the European Community whereby now France, now Britain, now West Germany, now Denmark is in the chair and there is a constant change of personnel. Frankly, I was very busy. I got a chance of promotion, and took it, even though I knew I wouldn't stay at the Berlaymont for much longer. Keith and I were now making busy wedding plans, and it looked as though the kind of job he wanted would materialize in Portugal. Kathy, my pleasant American flatmate had to return to California and write her thesis, and was replaced by another Irish girl, Mary O'Halloran.

In November, our cat, Bijou, was run over and killed, and it was then that I felt an era was at an end.

At Christmas, I had a card from Helena, posted from Morocco. 'All went well,' it said. 'Not to worry. Baby healthy, safely delivered and happily placed. Be happy!' At around the same time, an international delivery company fetched her remaining cases and shipped them to County Cork.

In the years that followed, I pieced together Helena's story. But then, in the years that followed, I was engrossed in my own life.

Keith and I went to Portugal after our marriage and we had a fascinating time. I look back on those early years of our marriage as honeyed. Keith loved the Portuguese and so did I. After being in the rather sophisticated, hothouse atmosphere of Brussels, Lisbon seemed old-fashioned and sweet. Our two eldest daughters were born there. Yes, thanks to my dear old Dutch cap, well-planned and well-spaced, too! We got back to the UK regularly, and I did my best to keep in touch with old friends from the Brussels network.

Towards the end of the seventies, there was talk of Portugal entering the Common Market, and I was invited to do some work for the European office which was set up in Lisbon.

Through this grapevine, little by little, I found out what had happened with Helena.

She had proceeded with the pregnancy, just as she said she would, and she had got in touch with Philippa Shields herself. Philippa was reluctant to meet her to begin with, but gradually came around to the idea. When they eventually got down to brass tacks, they had formed a remarkably practical team.

Helena had decided to have her baby in Morocco. Through her translating experience, she had developed contacts there and knew just how to organize it. Red tape matters much less in such countries; connections and *baksheesh* matter much more. If you bribe the right people, anything can be done.

Philippa had flown to Morocco at the time when Helena's baby was due. And she had returned, in due course, with Helena's baby, and with a full set of adoption papers. Six months later, the Irish authorities had ratified these Moroccan adoption documents, and Helena's baby was hers.

Helena had stayed in North Africa for a while, then returned to Ethiopia, where she also had work experience. She had got herself a job with the United Nations, working with famine relief. She became very committed to Third World charities in one form or another. She became especially committed to Third World charities helping poor children. Strangely enough, and perhaps appropriately enough, she also became an adviser to International Planned Parenthood, which helps poor people on birth control! She was hopeless at birth control herself, of course, but sometimes the people who fail at the ideal are the best at understanding.

Keith and I came back to England in 1983, when Keith got a job in Oxford, and I was invited to do a part-time job which involved getting Turkey into the European Community. Gosh! I smiled as I thought of Helena and the 'European spirit'. As I met good-looking, swarthy Turks, I imagined what fun she would have had with these gallants! They were gorgeous young men!

I haven't heard from Helena now for some years. Someone saw her in Nairobi and someone else saw her in Cuba. I'm sure she'll turn up again, one day. We will have a lot of gossip to exchange.

I have, however, heard from Philippa Shields. She always sends me a Christmas card. Last Christmas she sent me a picture of herself, with Mike, and their son, Philip. He's a fine young man – tall, sandy-haired, bespectacled. They're so proud of him.

Helena was such a wild girl. Crazy, funny, irresponsible. Yet she knew, instinctively, when she had gone too far, and she knew, too, when it was time to give to life what she had taken from it. In the end, she did a very honourable thing, and maybe the hardest thing that a woman *can* do: she gave a life, and walked away from it, leaving it to someone better fitted to nourish it.

I'm sure I'll hear from her again one day. I hope I will. I'd like to express my admiration. And the friendship I shall always feel for her.

Cinderella: Another Perspective

Once upon a time there was a poor widow called Mrs de Breffni. Mrs de Breffni was poor because she had been married to an Irishman of the greatest possible charm, and the least possible financial prudence. Indeed, Desmond de Breffni had scorned money, in the way that 'gentlemen' of his period often did. Money was 'trade', don't you know. The de Breffnis considered themselves to be *above* money.

Life in the 1940s and 1950s was very different from what it is in these days of Thatcher neo-capitalism when everyone thinks money is wonderful. In those post-war years, people in Ireland, however poor, affected not to think about money at all. Talking about money was the height of vulgarity. Land was all right. Education was all right. Style, culture and ancestor-worship were all right. But money was still kept firmly in the closet. Desmond de Breffni died in 1953, leaving a wife, two daughters, a notional if not entirely fictional barony which he had spent years tracing back to a Norman ancestor in County Clare, and a large Victorian house in Ballsbridge, Dublin which was more or less falling to pieces. And so his widow, Moira, found quite suddenly that while the society in which she lived appeared not to care for money, it made scant provision for poor widows without it.

If Moira de Breffni had enjoyed a well-connected, large or even very loyal family on her own side, things might have looked rosier for her. Unfortunately, Moira's own family was neither large nor well-connected nor even very loyal. She came from a modest Protestant background which had converted to Catholicism somewhat half-heartedly – for obscure marriage reasons – a generation back. The Protestant connections had practised birth control so effectively that the extended family had all but died out. Her own kinfolk consisted of one cantankerous aunt, and a cousin in County Meath who was distinctly odd.

There were some kinfolk on Desmond's side, but they were not close, partly because the generations were out of synchronization – Desmond's father had been very old when he married – and thus his own generation of cousins were all second cousins, sometimes second cousins once removed. Moreover, Desmond's father had taken a different side in the Irish Civil War to the rest of the family, which was another reason for a certain *froideur*. Desmond and his father were both by way of being radical, if erratic, Republicans, whereas the other de Breffnis were correct and churchy Free Staters. The rift had never been healed. So Moira de Breffni found herself alone in the world, with her two young daughters established at an expensive convent school; and no visible means of support.

Moira was, however, a sensible and resourceful woman, devoid of self-pity. After several private weeping sessions, she resolved to make the best of things, for herself and for her children. She could see, with a clear, unsentimental vision, that unless she did something constructive for herself, life would become oppressively frugal. Whatever eyewash society talks about the sanctity of motherhood and the care of widows and orphans, she noticed that the invitations to bridge parties and days out at Leopardstown races were no longer forthcoming to a widow down on her luck. With commendable energy, she went about turning her home in south Dublin into a boarding house for respectable persons requiring lodging. And this, she did, somehow, patching up the old house as best she could, prevailing upon local handymen to assist her with odd jobs, and finding that, when necessity pressed, she could drive quite a hard bargain.

And it was to her credit how well she managed during those hard times, running her home as a business enterprise, keeping her children on at the expensive convent school. She found herself able to persuade the nuns – notoriously capable businesswomen themselves – to accept slightly reduced fees, by the subtle and highly alarming means of declaring that she might be otherwise *obliged* to send her daughters to a Protestant school. Thus Moira learned the value of competition. She rose early in the morning and cooked breakfast for her six, seven, and sometimes eight, lodgers.

Most of her lodgers were agreeable people: a civil servant, a medical student, an accountant, a teacher, a pharmacist, a man who had an excellent job with Guinness, a bank employee, a Czech musician with the Radio Eireann orchestra. She made it a general rule not to take women lodgers because she felt that women were more of a moral, perhaps an emotional, responsibility; inclined to wash their smalls out in the bathroom, and also inclined to tell you their troubles, their troubles being so often the difficulty of finding a suitable husband, and then, possibly, setting their cap at one of the other lodgers. The exception was the schoolteacher, who was plain and middle-aged, and a cousin of her own eccentric County Meath cousin. Each lodger partook of a cooked breakfast in the morning, and then, at the end of the day, high tea. They each paid her twenty-five shillings a week, except for the schoolteacher who, on account of being a distant family connection, paid twenty-two and sixpence.

Moira's daughters, Francesca and Ludmilla, were extremely happy at the convent of the Holy Infant. They were sturdy, not to say stout, girls who were neither clever nor pretty, nor had, alas, much evidence of their father's legendary charm. But they entered into all enterprises with gusto, adored learning to play the piano (a little tunelessly perhaps), to speak French, to paint and to appreciate paintings, to practise their religion with all its May processions, its affecting veiling ceremonies: despite their reduced fees, the nuns found them gratifying pupils. They acted – not very convincingly, but with much enthusiasm – in the school plays, practised their elocution lessons the better to speak nicely in the drawing-rooms of south Dublin, and by the time they reached their teens, were well and truly filled with the airs and graces of young gentlewomen, while their mother scrubbed pots and pans in the old house's scullery. Each night, Moira would prepare the porridge for the following morning, a ritual which played sticky hell with saucepans in an age before the enlightened arrival of either instant oatflakes or efficient chemical cleaning-agents.

Francesca and Ludmilla were not, as we have said, gifted girls, but Moira loved them, and wanted to do everything that was best for them. And although they had not inherited their father's charm, they had, it seemed, inherited his lack of common sense when it came to money. In their teens, they begged to be permitted to learn to ride ponies, which, somehow, their self-sacrificing mother managed to arrange, although riding-lessons cost seven and sixpence an hour. The sisters were suited to ponies, as it turned out, being of a robust temperament and physique, unafraid of falling or being thrown – luckily, as they were thrown surprisingly frequently – and skilful at saddling and grooming the beasts. At home, they were inclined to be slothful around the house, and seldom lent their mother a hand; yet in the stables, they would do any job they were allocated. At that time, Moira's only steady domestic help was a good-tempered half-wit from County Kerry called Matty Butt, whom the girls sometimes referred to as Butty, or Buttons.

Buttons slept in an old shed at the back of the house which Moira had fixed up ingeniously: in later years, the shed was to fetch a pretty price in the Dublin real estate market as a 'studio flat'. Buttons was of an indeterminate age, slept in the renovated shed with his dog, Taffy, and gave Moira devoted service, having been rejected by his own family. He was an unlettered creature, but surprisingly capable at practical jobs, and was happy to look after the few hens that were kept in a little yard at the end of the generous garden.

The lodgers, of course, changed over the years. The medical

student graduated after taking his finals for the fourth time – he is now an esteemed heart specialist in Merrion Square, having discovered that a fine bedside manner more than compensated for the poor grasp of Latin pharmaceutical terms that had held him back academically. The bank clerk was transferred to Mullingar, and prospered too. The Czech musician died, a death hastened by his fondness for Irish whisky. The schoolteacher left after a difference with the civil servant. The pharmacist got married. Others came in their place, and whenever a new lodger arrived, Moira took the businesslike decision to increase her charges slightly. By such means, she was able to repair the old house a little more each year, to install a telephone, even to purchase that wonderful luxury, a washing-machine.

In 1958, Mrs de Breffni acquired a very personable lodger called Captain Bruce-Anderson.

Captain Bruce-Anderson was indeed a person of allure. He was a widower himself, from an old Scottish Highland Catholic family and clearly every inch a gentleman. It was uncertain quite how and why he found himself in Dublin, having retired early from his regiment, but it was understood that he had some vague business interests in Ireland. There was a kindness and a polish about the Captain that was irresistible. Unlike the other lodgers, he would help to clear away the china after high tea. He made his own bed. His room was immaculate, and his shoes always in perfect condition, if a little worn. He was tactful. He sat in his room reading books when it was appropriate to respect Moira's privacy, but he kept her company at moments when she appreciated it. It was only when he talked to her, while she caught up with the sewing, that she realized just how much she did appreciate such company.

During the school holidays, Captain Bruce-Anderson disappeared off to England, where his young daughter, Ella, dwelt. Ella was installed in a boarding-school in Berkshire, and during the holidays she stayed with the Captain's sister, who was a married lady living near Cheltenham, and who, according to the Captain, greatly doted on the young niece who had lost her own mother at a tender age. Captain Bruce-Anderson managed to spend that holiday-time with his sister and daughter, but he continued to pay Moira scrupulously for the retention of his room.

Moira grew to like and respect the Captain a great deal. If he took a little too much brandy and soda now and again, well, that was a gentleman's privilege. He was never offensive in drink. She often felt the urge to give him two eggs for breakfast, rather than the regulation singleton. She took to darning his socks and replacing the buttons on his Jermyn Street shirts. And one pleasant May afternoon, when they were sitting in the garden eating ice-cream, she realized that she had grown exceedingly fond of him.

Having earned her living and supported her family so effectively, Moira had also grown in self-confidence and what we would now call, perhaps, assertiveness. It does something to a woman, having to be the man of the family, and Moira had gradually learned that if you want something, you must be energetic in pursuing it.

'Are you hoping to stay in Ireland?' she asked the Captain.

'Oh rather. I think so,' the Captain replied. 'I love it here.'

There was a slight pause. Then Moira said, her heart beating hard with her own boldness: 'Have you ever considered marrying again, Captain?'

He stirred. 'To be absolutely honest, Mrs de Breffni,' he replied, 'I don't have the means. I can just about survive on my pension and on my little business ventures, but support a wife . . . alas, no.'

In those days, dear reader, men believed they had no right to marry unless they could support a wife, and a potential family.

Moira rooted through her sewing-basket distractedly. 'I think,' she said, 'that at this stage, I *have* the means for such a marriage, if you wish to look at it that way.'

He regarded her in astonishment.

'I couldn't possibly . . .'

'I don't see why not. We could easily make this house a business together.'

The Captain turned his face away, momentarily. He was moved by the suggestion. He looked at the pear tree, at the garden which was so restful, at the birds tweeting away overhead. He looked back at Moira, whose eyes were full of affection for him.

'My dear,' he said, tenderly. 'If I thought for a moment that you would consent to have me for a husband, I would consider myself a very lucky man.'

She smiled. 'Then in that case, my dear Jack, you are!' She rose and went inside the house, returning with a bottle of brandy and two glasses, as a gesture of celebration.

The news of the impending wedding was greeted with the worst possible show of temper by Francesca and Ludmilla. 'Mother – how *could* you?' asked Ludmilla, aghast. The girl thought that her mother had taken leave of her senses. Marrying again, at the age of forty-two! What was the point? People of forty-two, *women* of forty-two were past all that sort of thing! It wasn't decent! 'What would Father have thought?' chimed in Francesca, who had been her father's particular pet.

In truth, Francesca and Ludmilla intensely disliked the idea of sharing their mother with someone else. They had had her to themselves for so long, now.

Moira was painting the kitchenette – a store-room and pantry next to the scullery – at the time of the crisis. 'Don't worry, darlings,' she said soothingly, for she was always inclined to indulge her daughters. 'Nothing will change – except that we will be a real family again. We'll all get along grandly. Captain Jack is very fond of you both.'

But the pair, now seventeen and eighteen, sulked and pouted. 'I sincerely hope that it is not going to change our lives,' said Ludmilla. 'I suppose,' Francesca pointed out, 'this daughter of Jacko's is going to join our new big happy family?'

Moira hadn't given this matter much thought, but she now

reflected on it. 'I am sure that Captain Jack's daughter will fit in very well,' she said. As Jack was such a nice man, his daughter was bound to be pleasant, too. 'She's around your age – it will be nice to have someone else young around the house. That is, if she comes to live here. She may not. After all, she's accustomed to being with her aunt.'

The wedding took place at the beginning of August, and as was still the tradition, the catering was to be done at home. Moira engaged some friends from the Irish Country Ladies' Institute to organize the wedding breakfast. The Country Ladies' Institute specialized in all domestic skills, and Moira had learned much from her own involvement in the organization. There was, however, a prodigious amount to do for the wedding breakfast, and it did occur to Moira at the time that there was a potential market for such affairs on a commercial basis. Wedding catering could be such a useful service, she thought, if carried out on a professional basis.

Still, it was a happy party. There was a marquee in the garden, and as the nuns at the convent of the Holy Infant had prayed to St Clare for a fine day, a fine day duly dawned. Captain Bruce-Anderson and Mrs de Breffni were married in a quiet ceremony – as befitted their widowed state – at University Church, Dublin, and after the reception, departed for a short honeymoon in Killarney.

Mrs Tweedie, an organising member of the Irish Country Ladies' Association, kindly agreed to look after the lodgers for a week, while Francesca and Ludmilla went and stayed with some horsey friends in Kildare.

The Captain's daughter, Ella, came over from England for the occasion, accompanied by her aunt. She was a fragile-looking girl, very pretty. She clung rather poignantly to her father, whenever she could be with him, and was disinclined to mix with the Irish faction. Hostilities with Francesca and Ludmilla were immediately established, unfortunately, when she ventured to say she disliked horses as rough beasts. She gave the impression, too, that in marrying in Ireland her father was allying himself with a barbarous tribe. Paradoxically, however, she took an instant liking to Matty Butt, whost antics amused her greatly. Moira thought they both seemed orphans, somehow.

The honeymoon was blissful. It was a joy, a delight, a pleasure of immense worth for Moira to have a husband again, and Jack Bruce-Anderson proved as sweet in intimacy as he had been in friendship. He revealed a droll side of his nature. He smelled of soap and tobacco; he bristled with masculine attractions. If he took a little too much brandy in the evening, he was full of desire in the morning. It was heaven.

They returned to Dublin, presently, to resume their ordinary lives. The plan was that Moira would continue to run her boarding house on the practical lines she had so well established, with a view to turning it eventually into a proper hotel; Jack would continue with his own business interests – he dabbled somewhat on the stock exchange – and oversee the accounts of the house. His daughter, Ella, would come and live in Dublin for part of the time – having finished at her school – and pursue a cooking course at a Dublin catering college. But she would be free to stay with her aunt in Cheltenham, too, when that suited her.

These plans were straight away upset by the aunt's sudden change of circumstances.

Out of the blue, her husband had a lucrative opportunity to go and work in Hong Kong. The house in Cheltenham was to be rented, while the aunt and uncle went to live in the Far East. Ella would have to accompany them, or to come to Ireland and live with her father and step-mother. And so she chose to come to Ireland, disliking the thought of Hong Kong even more than Ireland.

Moira had hoped that in resuming the status of a married lady – from having been a hard-working widow – she might again take up some of the leisure pursuits she had once enjoyed: bridge, the races, the visiting of art galleries and the purchase, sometimes, of paintings. However, she soon discovered that her husband, while an adorable man in so many respects, was, like Desmond de Breffni, not a practical person. People often marry a second partner remarkably like their first, and so Jack Bruce-Anderson proved to be; charming, good company, considerate and kind. But again, without that practical sense for finance that Moira had discovered was necessary for prosperity and self-improvement. Once again, she wasted no time in bemoaning her lot, but sensibly set about improving it. With great tact, she made sure that Jack made no serious financial decisions on her part. And when a derelict hotel came up for sale on a prime site in Dublin, she managed to persuade her bank manager to advance her a loan to buy it. As a widow and on her own, she might have had difficulties in doing this. But as a married woman, and with a man at her side, she found it possible. She bought it and threw herself into turning it into a viable business, using the knowledge that she had built up from the modest beginnings of her lodging-house.

For more than two years, life went on thus. Mrs Tweedie was now engaged as a full-time housekeeper in their own home. Ludmilla and Francesca, still horse-mad, nevertheless did secretarial courses in Dublin with a view to earning their living. Ella completed her course in *cordon bleu* cooking at the Dublin school of catering, sometimes going to Hong Kong during the holidays, when her aunt sent her the fare. Jack went about his own business, and did wonders in the garden.

Moira did her best to be civil to her step-daughter, but in truth, they didn't really hit it off. Ella was withdrawn, moody, even sly, with her. It was true that she was helpful about the house: she liked domesticity, unlike Ludmilla and Francesca. She got on wonderfully with Matty Butt. They were forever larking and giggling together, and devising silly tricks for the dog.

Then again, Moira was often so busy that she didn't always have *time* to communicate – either with Ella or with her own daughters. The new hotel took up much of her concentration and energies, and she had launched this new idea of hosting wedding parties there. There was a terrific demand for the facility. Then she found a second hotel in the Dun Laoghaire area. The bank manager was so impressed by her management of the first one that he readily advanced her a further loan for the second. Moira's reputation as a capable – and sometimes tough – businesswoman was growing.

Francesca and Ludmilla completed their secretarial courses. They were both huge girls now. Moira thought, when she looked at them, that they'd make perfect wives for farmers – so healthy, buxom and strong. They continued to be horse-mad, and, although they scarcely made faultless secretaries, they were both shrewd enough to get themselves jobs in the horsey world. Ludmilla worked for the Horse Show department of the Royal Dublin Society, while Ludmilla procured a job with the Irish Bloodstock Sales Company.

Just as Ella had graduated from her cookery course, and was mooning about the house, as was her wont, wondering what to do next, Jack Bruce-Anderson suffered a frightening heart attack. He was taken into hospital immediately, where, before anything could be done, he had a second crisis and died. Moira immediately cut short a catering conference she was attending in Cork at the time and rushed to his bedside. He died in her arms. She wept as bitter tears over her second husband as over her first. Except that this time, she had the experience to cope with it.

Widowed once again, Moira once again buried herself in her work. She took time off to attend a hotelier training course in Switzerland – which some people thought was heartless of her, in her grief, but which she knew was necessary. The hotel business was growing, expanding, as was tourism. This was the 1960s. You had to be professional.

She developed a strong public image. When Irish television started in 1961, she readily appeared on TV programmes talking about catering and tourism. In her middle forties now, she began to grow stout, which somehow reinforced her public persona as a strong woman. She took courses in wine appreciation, and hired chefs who produced excellent food.

77

Moira suggested to Ella that she might like to go and work in her main Dublin hotel, the Edmund Burke, as a woman chef – an innovatory idea at the time, when all chefs were men. But Ella was diffident. She said she didn't like the rough world of commercialism. She preferred, she said, to stay at home in Ballsbridge, with Mrs Tweedie and Buttons. The house had been renovated now, and there were only three lodgers left.

It was now no longer necessary to keep them, but Moira allowed them to stay on until they made other arrangements. However, as facilities had been consistently improved – there were now three toilets and two bathrooms in the old house, a living-room with a television, and two telephones – she felt justified in increasing her weekly charges to five pounds, and then five guineas.

Years afterwards, Moira reproached herself for not giving more attention to Ella, or for not trying harder to reconcile her own daughters with her step-daughter. But at the time, Moira was so busy in her business affairs, there seldom seemed an opportunity for such niceties. Moira, too, grew impatient with people who had to be cajoled and looked after. Nobody is successful at everything, and Moira had found that she was able to be successful in business. Who was to blame her if she wasn't always successful in understanding young people?

Things came to a head, in a way, with the Dublin Horse Show ball of 1962. Ludmilla and Francesca were all of a-twitter in anticipation of it. The Dublin Horse Show – traditionally held in the first week of August – had come to be the fulcrum of the fashionable season for the English and Irish grandees. Smart young things did the London season in the spring, followed by the English sporting events of early summer – the Oxford and Cambridge boat race, the Henley regatta, the May balls, the debs dances, and finished up at the Dublin Horse Show. The 'season' closed on 12 August, the 'Glorious Twelfth' when the men dispersed to shoot grouse in Scotland.

Ludmilla and Francesca planned their schedule with their

usual enthusiasm. Frocks were bought at Brown Thomas, and then, inevitably, altered by the trusted dressmaker, Mrs O'Reilly, since they always had to be let out. The pair of them derived no end of pleasure from the anticipation of the week of parties, and their mother thought it a harmless pursuit. She was so involved with yet another hotel deal – this one in Belfast, no less – that she paid no great attention to her daughters. Mrs Tweedie was more excited by the Horse Show Ball than she was.

To Moira, now a fully engaged career woman, it didn't seem that significant. It never crossed her mind that this could be the most exciting occurrence in the lives of the young people in her home.

Francesca and Ludmilla were especially animated by the rumour that a stunning Polish aristocrat, Prince Charles Zamoyski, was coming to Dublin for the ball. Prince Charles was, according to reputation, tall, handsome, fair-haired, and looked just like Tab Hunter, a film star of the time. He was, as it happened, half-American, since his father, Prince Zyismunt, had had the good judgment to marry an American cornflake millionairess. Thus the Prince was all at once handsome, rich, and Roman Catholic, the last characteristic putting him at a slight disadvantage with the English and Irish Protestant gentry, but making him greatly desirable to Catholic girls of good family. Although aristocrats fussed slightly less about religion in those days than the common people, they still fussed a little nevertheless.

Moira was inclined to smile at her daughters' gossiping about the Prince. She was far too realistic to imagine that they would be candidates for such a match. She still felt they would do well to find farmers who liked healthy girls who understood horses. Occasionally, she had caught herself reading the lonely-hearts columns of the Irish provincial publications – usually in the course of searching the property pages – and noted how often farmers stipulated that prospective wives should be healthy. Knowing the state of Irish farms, and the amount of physical work involved, she considered that quite fair.

Ludmilla and Francesca, however, had no such thoughts of sensible farmers. They were all for Romance. They would learn, Moira reflected.

Just as it didn't cross her busy mind that the Horse Show Ball was all that important for her daughters, neither did it occur to her that it might be something her step-daughter, Ella, would wish to attend. Ella had always made plain her strong dislike of horses, and, by extension, the horsey crowd. So, to begin with, the question of Ella going to the ball didn't arise. It was just thought of as very much Francesca's and Ludmilla's scene – but not Ella's.

Mrs Tweedie, however, thought differently. She had gradually come to regard Ella as a most neglected young person. Here she was, such a pretty girl, nineteen years old, and no one ever bothered about her. She played with the dog, she played with the cat, she was obliging about the house, she confided in Buttons. She was reserved, Mrs Tweedie realized, because she was English. The English were like that. They didn't go around telling people their woes. They weren't like Irish folk, blathering away at the tops of their voices, but that didn't mean they didn't have feelings. Poor Ella. It wasn't fair.

And it was, indeed, to Mrs Tweedie that Ella shyly confessed that she would have liked to go to the big ball. Wistfully, bashfully, she made her thoughts known. Mrs Tweedie's maternal feelings came immediately to the fore when she heard this, as she declared: 'Well, in that case, my dear, you *shall* go to the ball!' Ella and Mrs Tweedie were cleaning the silver together when this avowal was made.

Jill Tweedie soon set about organizing Ella's ticket for the grand Dublin Horse Show ball. She had a nephew working at the Royal Dublin Society, and by the judicious use of bribery, she pressed him to procure a ticket. She also got the most wonderful ball-gown on loan, though a connection who worked with Sybil Connelly, the top dress designer. She even finangled the hire of a carriage – a beautiful white Rolls Royce which belonged to one of the older members of the Irish Country Ladies' Institute, the rich widow of a wine merchant called Mrs Morgan. Mrs Morgan was generous – a great patroness of animal charities – but eccentric. She said that they *could* have the use of the car, yes, but it must be back in the garage by 12.30 a.m. on the dot. Her chauffeur was taking her to Donegal the next day, and she stipulated that he must not be kept up: he must do his last job at midnight and get the car garaged thirty minutes later. Mrs Tweedie promised.

All these arrangements were made in a spirit of great conspiracy. Jill Tweedie took it on herself to be Ella's fairy godmother for the evening; it was nothing to do with Moira. Ludmilla and Francesca were not to be told, either. They would only start quarrelling and being awkward. The only person who was party to the enterprise was Matty Butt, who was beside himself with glee at the prospect of his adored Ella being treated like a princess.

Anyway, Moira was away for the evening in question. She had taken a trip to London to look at new kitchen technology.

The August evening was soft and balmy when Ludmilla and Francesca went off with their noisy escorts, screeching with laughter and squeezed into an MG sports car. Half an hour later, the white Rolls Royce drew up in front of the Ballsbridge house, with its commission to fetch Ella. Ella appeared at the front door, the picture of loveliness. Her dress was soft, white and simple, unlike the whaleboned frocks of the time which dug into a girl's bosom. She looked very vulnerable. Her long hair cascaded down on her shoulders, in an era when all smart girls wore short, bouffant hairstyles.

Matty Butt was close to tears as he pressed a flower on Ella. She accepted it, looking at him with feeling. Taffy the dog barked in appreciation. Mrs Tweedie felt proud at what she had wrought. 'Don't forget, Ella,' she said. 'Leave at midnight.' Ella nodded silently. She moved off as though in a dream.

It was left to the Dublin evening papers to tell the story of Ella's triumph the next afternoon. 'The Belle of the Ball!' they captioned the photographs. 'Mysterious blonde dances with Prince – and disappears!' 'Teenage beauty in mercy dash from dance!' One paper had concocted a report to the effect that Ella had dazzled the ball, and then disappeared at midnight to care for a sick relative. Several pictures showed her in the arms of Prince Charles Zamoyski, who looked captivated. He also looked captivated when dancing with several other young ladies, it should be said.

All Moira discovered, when she flew back to Dublin the following evening, was that Ella's picture had been in the paper, and that her daughters were in somewhat bad form. Moira was quite innocently pleased to see Ella's picture, and thought no more about it. She had had a very successful London trip, and had bought some excellent new kitchen equipment. She had also had a couple of delicious Asian meals in London, and was considering opening a curry restaurant in Dublin. Why not? It was good, cheap food, and piquantly different.

Moira had developed the habit of not asking her daughters too closely about their romantic affairs. She had learned the wisdom of all mothers – that daughters tell you what they want to tell you in their own good time. And if they are questioned too closely, they are apt to rebuff an enquiring parent. So she made no special fuss about the ball, and waited, politely, until information was volunteered.

The information, when it came, came in a curious way. There was a telephone call, two days after Moira arrived home, from Prince Charles Zamoyski. It happened at around six o'clock in the evening. Moira took the call and the Prince introduced himself politely.

'May I call upon you later this evening, Mrs Bruce-Anderson?' he asked.

'To be sure,' Moira answered. 'It would be a pleasure to receive you.' Perhaps, it occurred to her, he was interested in investing in her hotel chain. She might, after all, go public in the near future. Investors could be welcome.

'I think someone in your family has lost something, and I

would like to return it,' he added. His American accent was light; there was a European formality in the way he spoke.

'Please call by,' she said. 'Come about eight.'

She gave him the address.

The family had supper nowadays in their private dining-room; the guests ate now in another place. Over the family meal, Moira mentioned that Prince Charles Zamoyski would be calling by. Ludmilla and Francesca went into a frenzy. 'Why didn't you tell us, Mother?' they cried. And they rushed off to pretty themselves for the occasion. Ella, meanwhile, went off to play ping-pong with Matty Butt in the games room – an extension of his studio shed in the garden.

The doorbell rang at around eight fifteen. Marie-Christine, the French student who was staying in the house as a part-time mother's help, admitted the visitors and showed them into the upstairs drawing-room. Moira came immediately to greet her guests.

The Prince was accompanied by a young Negro, fastidiously dressed. 'This is my assistant, Mr George Dubois,' the Prince said. 'I am your humble servant, Charles Zamoyski.'

The Prince kissed Moira's hand, just as her second husband had done, in the garden, when she had proposed to him. George Dubois bowed over her hand, full of Louisiana courtesies.

'I'm delighted to see you,' Moira said, naturally. 'Make yourselves at home. What would you like – sherry, whisky, brandy, a gin?' Irish hospitality included liquor and so liquor immediately was offered.

The Prince hesitated. 'Perhaps a glass of wine?' he suggested. 'To be sure,' said Moira, and went to the top of the stairs, where she could see Marie-Christine. She asked the girl to go to the cellar and fetch a cool bottle of Muscadet.

'I hope you're enjoying your stay in Ireland,' she chatted away to the Prince, as they awaited Marie-Christine's wine delivery.

'Enormously,' said the Prince.

'A wonderful country,' echoed George Dubois.

'Do you have horses here?' was the natural next question.

'I'm certainly thinking of acquiring some.'

'My daughter works with the Bloodstock people – she can guide you about sales. A cigarette?' Moira opened the silver cigarette box.

Both gentlemen declined.

Marie-Christine brought the wine, which was cool, but not chilled.

After a moment, George Dubois began the business in hand. 'We have a piece of jewellery here,' he said, 'which belongs to a young lady in your household.' He opened a small box to reveal an ear-ring. 'The Prince would like to return it to the young lady, and to match it with the one she possesses.'

Moira looked at it. It seemed just like an ordinary pearl ear-ring. 'Well, yes, both my daughters have ear-rings like that. I daresay they'll be glad to claim them.' She smiled brightly and went out of the room again. She called to Marie-Christine. 'Marie-Christine! Can you tell the girls – Ludmilla and Francesca – to come and join us?'

The two young women were swift in their response, and bounded into the drawing-room with their usual gusto, their moon-faces covered with a gaudy application of make-up.

'Prince Charles!' gushed Ludmilla. 'How super to see you!' Francesca was equally effusive.

The Prince was courteous, but George Dubois was clearly in charge of the business in hand. He showed the girls the ear-ring and asked if they could match it.

At first, they protested that they could, to be sure, it was just a pearl ear-ring like any other. Then Mr Dubois pointed out that it was an ear-ring that would only fit a pierced ear. Did they have pierced ears? Ludmilla and Francesca looked at one another. No, they didn't have pierced ears. It was considered rather common, at that time, and rather foreign, too, to pierce one's ears.

Moira spoke up. 'I think my step-daughter uses pierced ear-rings,' she said.

'May we see your step-daughter?' asked George Dubois.

'Of course,' said Moira, feeling uncomfortable, for no good reason she could think of. 'Ludmilla, go and ask Ella to come and join us.'

Sulkily, Ludmilla went to fetch her step-sister, who was still in the games-shed with Buttons. When she entered the drawing room, she was wearing, in one ear, the perfect match of the small pearl that George had in the box.

'Goodness me,' Ella exclaimed shyly when she saw its pair. 'I must have lost that at the Horse Show dance. The little gadget that holds it in at the back went adrift.'

George Dubois held up a small stopper. 'We have found a replacement for it,' he said, triumphally. He fitted the ear-ring to her ear: a perfect match for the one already in place.

They had a cordial evening, on the whole, with the Prince and Ella exchanging curiously enchanted glances. The courtship was pursued and before too long the marriage was announced between Prince Charles Zamoyski and Miss Gabriella Bruce-Anderson.

Although she had never got along very well with her step-daughter, Moira was quite pleased. Although Ludmilla and Francesca grumbled about Ella's sly ways, they were reconciled to the engagement, eventually.

Mrs Tweedie took proprietorial glee in the match, and Matty Butt was ecstatic. After her marriage, Ella developed into a much fuller person; she lost the shyness and the slyness that had made her so difficult to communicate with, so impenetrable. She was, quite simply, a woman born to be a wife, and although Prince Charles Zamoyski had his little failings – all husbands do, do they not? – they nevertheless *lived happily ever after*.

Why I Am a Feminist

You ask me why I am a feminist? Well, who isn't! You've got to be, nowadays, when you look at the lives women lead. And the lives that women *have* led, in the past. Shocking. I was a feminist from the year dot. Born with a clenched fist, you might say. Right on! They were my first words! No, seriously, I never remember *not* feeling angry about women's rights, or, rather, the lack of them. I'm forty-eight and I'm still angry.

The usual textbook feminist is angry with her Father. I know. I've read – not Freud, no, but the post-Freudians on it. Germaine Greer – furious with her father. That's the classic psycho-pathology for feminists, apparently. Little girl rebels against Daddy, Daddy represents *all* male authority, little girl wants to overturn all male authority. There's probably something about penis-envy in there too – there usually is. But I'm not textbook in this respect. My feminist formation came from a completely different source. Not my father. Not my mother. My *aunts*. There's a new one for the sociologists. 'The role of the aunt in inner-city kinship structures.' The English, of course, don't have aunties – not blood aunties – any more. You need large families to produce a crop of aunts, because you always have to allow for wastage: one goes into the loony bin, one goes to Australia – same thing, you might say. You can't really raise a rich crop of aunts from families with 1.5 children. The English had aunts by the dozen in Victorian times, and the Irish, of course, actually had Victorian times until about 1975.

So I was formed by my aunts.

You see, my mother died when I was a small child. She was what they used to call 'delicate'. That means she had tuberculosis. Actually, she *didn't* die from TB, because by the 1940s they were curing it. But it must have weakened her health. She died from something they called 'galloping pneumonia'.

I was not quite five at the time, so I don't really remember what happened, but the stories I heard afterwards were terrible. She was literally chilled to the bone. No matter how many blankets she was given, she could not get warm. I remember nothing about it, exactly, yet the older I get, the more I think of her suffering, and how awful it must have been for her to leave two young children behind. People accepted suffering in those days. Especially, I should add, suffering by women. *That* was a woman's role. To suffer. Look at the Sacred Heart of Mary, they used to say – pierced through with a sword. Woman's lot. They tried to get you trained in early, thinking like this.

This is weird, but no one told me that my mother was dead. I was fobbed off with excuses about her being in hospital, until, of course, a playmate informed me, rather mockingly. I remember the precise moment, the precise part of the garden in which we were playing, the gloating look in this noxious child's eyes as she said to me: *you* think your mammy is just sick, but she's not, she's *dead* – so there! Oh, childhood is a rehearsal for life. They say children are cruel, but children are only as cruel as people in general. Adults are just slightly more devious and sly in their cruelties. I remember that moment, and knowing it was the truth, and knowing that somewhere I had suspected it. I have had many other moments like that in life, when a truth was revealed to me, and then I knew that I had known it all along. When Jonathan told me he was leaving me, that he had decided to 'come out of the closet' and form a gay relationship, I had exactly the same sensation as I had back in that Dublin garden: I had known, unconsciously, and the spoken word only served to bring it to light. Marriage is a farce, isn't it? I'm glad now that Jonathan left. I hope he gets AIDS –

and by the way he cruised for a while, he deserves to – and I'm still glad we split up. It's enabled me to see life as it is. Bitterly.

Anyway, soon after my mother died, I went to live with one of my numerous aunts. My father was a nice man, actually, but academic and vague. My elder brother was already at boarding school, at the age of eight. So I was packed off to Aunty Eithne, who was married to Uncle Gerry.

It wasn't much of a trauma at the time because Aunty Eithne and Uncle Gerry lived very near what had been my parents' home, so there was no melodramatic transition. Aunty Eithne was my father's sister, but the complete opposite to him in personality. Where he was the absent-minded professor, she was rivettingly down to earth. The best housewife in Rathmines – everyone said so. You could eat your dinner off her kitchen floor. Her kitchen floor was often pointed to as an exemplar of what a kitchen floor should look like – scrubbed and spotless and shining, like one of those horrible adverts on TV for some blasted cleaning chemical.

Aunty Eithne's kitchen floor was spotless and clean and immaculate because that was what she spent her life doing. There wasn't an inch of that Victorian house in south Dublin that wasn't cleaned and scrubbed and polished half to death. Polishing brasses and stair-rods, silver, wooden parquets, beating carpets, cleaning out the 'charming' old range, polishing fenders and doorknobs and knockers, beeswaxing furniture, staining tiles, *besides* washing and airing and ironing and cooking and washing-up and putting away, and all the other dreary, boring, *drudgery* of housework in the days of rudimentary domestic technology. Housework is slavery! From the earliest age it struck me: here is a woman beating a carpet, and next week it will be dusty again! Here is a woman with a dedicated round of chores which are undone as soon as they are done! Wilberforce abolished slavery, but not for the domestic slaves known as housewives. It was terrible, I thought then, and I still think now. I would rather live and die a slut than live the life of a houseproud woman: maybe that's why I am a slut, mind you. You should see the state of my flat. And having four cats doesn't help. But I would rather sleep under Charing Cross Bridge, as God is my witness – wait a minute, I don't believe in God, do I? – well *façon de parler*. I would rather sleep rough and free than live in a clean home and be a prisoner called a housewife.

Now, I won't say that Aunty Eithne was forced into this frame of mind. She wasn't. Not overtly, anyway. Her husband, Uncle Gerry, was a mild man who made few demands. He had his own business and took the responsibility of providing for her seriously, although they had no children – perhaps *because* they had no children. Childless couples are notoriously more conscientious. It wasn't Uncle Gerry forcing Aunty Eithne to make herself a domestic drudge. It was something in herself. I think it is a way that women internalize their sense of inferiority – an inferiority that is taught to them. They think so little of themselves that they feel they can only win some kind of social invisible approval by having an exquisitely clean house.

It certainly wasn't that she enjoyed it. She *hated* it. She often told me so. 'God send the day,' she used to say, 'when we will all eat pills. No more shopping. No more cooking. No more washing up.' She lived just long enough to see the development of the space programme and it thrilled her to learn that the astronauts fed off chemicals and food compounds when they were circling the earth! To her, the space programme was pioneering the day when people would not need to be cooked for! Yet, ironically, she was a wonderful cook. A wonderful plain cook. Steak-and-kidney pie, fresh salmon *en croûte*, gooseberry fool, Bakewell tart, a perfect Yorkshire pudding, fish soup . . . then soda bread, cakes, jams, jellies. She did everything with diligence. I wish I had asked her for her special mayonnaise recipe. I shall never have it now. It was like a light, fluffy, sour cream – perfect. Oh, her diligence gave pleasure to others, to be sure. When she died, everything in her household was still immaculate: the sheets ironed and folded in the linen cupboard, which smelt of lavender: everything down to her handkerchiefs in mint condition, washed and pressed. Her tablecloths were all in fine repair – she never neglected her needlework, needless to say. Her home was her monument.

And yet, I asked myself – is this *worth a woman's life?* Aunty Eithne was a capable person. She might have done a lot of other things, rather than just be a housewife. Of course, I suppose she did do this: she helped to make me a feminist by negative example. I saw the toll on her nerves, the toll of domestic drudgery. And she always told me that the most important goal in a woman's life was to have some financial independence. 'What's his is mine,' she would say. 'And what's mine is my own. *Always* keep your own resources.' She left me £10,000. I bought my first flat with it. She'd have been appalled, all the same, by the state I kept it in!

I would spend the school terms with Aunty Eithne and Uncle Gerry; but I'd often visit the other aunts during the school holidays, which were gloriously long in my childhood. Three months in the summer. A month at Christmas. Nearly a month at Easter. I had two aunts on my mother's side who were blood relations, and then a few more of them married to uncles on Pa's side. There were also some great-aunts.

My mother was one of three sisters. Beauties, all three. Dark hair, blue eyes, pointed little chins. The true Irish colleens. White skin – the 'delicate' type, I suppose. My mother's two sisters were Aunty Florence and Aunty May. I was very fond of Aunty Florence because she reminded me so much of my mother in a straight animal, biological way. She *smelt* like my mother, or so I fancied. They were close in age and they had been close in attachment. So there was a whole feeling of the echoing of characteristics. My father used to say that Aunty Florence's voice was so like my mother's that it was eerie for him.

Aunty Florence was sweet, but my God, she had a terrible life, too. She was married to a monster. A *monster.* Uncle Matt. The original Male Chauvinist Pig. He wouldn't let her do anything. She wasn't allowed to shop, for example. He didn't trust her with money. 'You silly little butterfly-brain,' he'd say to her. 'The shopkeepers would have you robbed!' So he ordered all the provisions from the local grocer and they were delivered every day. Yes, in the 1940s and 50s, that's what Dublin grocers did: they delivered! And Aunty Flo didn't have the price of a pair of stockings herself, unless she asked him for it. He must have felt a terrific sense of power over that woman! He just controlled her in every conceivable way. She was not allowed to drive a car. She was not allowed to take a glass of sherry – oh, yes, he was a teetotaller. And how!

He was a fanatical member of an organization called the Pioneer Association which campaigned aggressively against alcohol, mawkishly displaying a bleeding heart symbol in order to advertise themselves. All children of my generation were more or less forced to take the Pioneer pledge at the age of about eight. All this appealed to Uncle Matt because he was a deeply authoritarian man: his main impetus in life was controlling people, particularly women, and particularly *his* womenfolk. The masculine mystique: authority and control. I hated him. Though of course, needless to say, he was a very handsome man – the kind of big, good-looking brute a certain kind of woman goes for; the kind of woman, I suspect, who likes, or who has been conditioned to like, bastards.

For one reason or another, Aunty Flo was that kind of lady. A doormat. Actually, she was an artist at heart – she would have been a gentle, flower-child and Bohemian in another age, and in a less repressed society. If she had married a man who encouraged her talent – instead of suppressing her and sneering at her creativity – she might have become an accomplished painter. As things were, he refused to allow her to go to the Dublin College of Art, which she wanted to do once her children were in school. 'I *know* what goes on in those so-called art classes,' he said in a sinister voice, rustling the newspaper irksomely. Nothing more was said, but Aunty Flo looked wretched. Apparently, Uncle Matt was referring to the very occasional sessions when students drew from life – that is, using a nude model. That was Uncle Matt all over. Narrow as all get-out. Listen to this. He asked the nuns at the school where his children went to draw little inky dresses over the naked African women in the National Geographic Magazine. Did you ever! I think it was the idea that women might actually be free enough to go around naked that upset him more than anything else, for he was an avowed opponent of individual freedom, especially women's freedom.

He had pots of money – he was a doctor, but there was family money, too. But he kept very strict accounts. Sometimes, Aunty Flo would get a few quid from her mother, or from some of her aunts. He would cross-examine her relentlessly about the way she might spend this. There was a time when she bought a hat for nine guineas at Switzer's. There was great carry-on about that. 'Nine pounds, nine shillings!' he'd shaken his head. 'On a silly hat!' He then denounced Switzer's as 'a Protestant shop'. If she had to throw money away, why couldn't she use Clery's, and give the money to Catholic shopkeepers? That was the way he thought.

I would have thought that the happiest day of Aunty Flo's life would be when this repellent bully dropped off the perch. Liberation at last. But life's a sod, sometimes. She didn't survive him more than three or four months. She had just begun to enjoy a little glass of sherry for herself, and had even made some tentative plans for a Mediterranean cruise which would take in the artistic high spots of the ancient world, when she collapsed and was rushed to hospital. She died a week later from something called hypercalcium, which I believe conceals some form of cancer. She was spared a long illness, but poor dear, Aunty Flo – to die, without really having lived at all! And yet, I was told that her last words were – 'I loved him, you know. I loved him very much.' She *loved* that bugger. Women are fools.

I made up my mind, when I was quite young, that I would never be trapped like Aunty Flo – trapped in a despotic marriage that was without personal freedom, without intellectual or creative development. I remember thinking then that I didn't want to get married at all – for look what marriage had brought to my aunts: drudgery, repression, imprisonment. I wish I had stuck to my resolution, though of course my own marriage was so short-lived it is almost as if I haven't been married at all.

I have that hat of Aunty Flo's, by the way – the one she spent nine guineas on. Sometimes I look at it and think: 'I'll avenge you, poor Flo: on the whole sodding race of men!'

You ask me why I am a feminist. But is it any wonder, when you think of the society I grew up in: Catholic Ireland in the 1940s and 50s. Feudal. Yes, I will have another vodka, as you're asking. Make it a double. I haven't told you about Aunty Delia yet. That's the cruncher.

Delia wasn't a blood aunt. She was married to one of my father's brothers, Uncle Paddy. Now Uncle Paddy was one of these 'patriotic game' types. Irish politics breakfast, dinner and tea. A nice man, actually, in certain respects – he had the same bent for scholarship as my father – and he could be funny. But when it came to politics – forget it! He would bore the hind legs off a donkey talking about Irish history and all the terrible wrongs that had been done to 'the most distressful country that ever yet was seen'. If he was alive today, he'd be in the IRA, and of course in his way he probably contributed to the fortunes of the IRA, because he was a teacher, and he probably taught generations of boys this poisonous nationalism. That's another great masculine mystique. Killing people. Putting bombs under school buses and calling that 'the armed struggle'. Killing lonely Protestant farmers in County Armagh and going to America as a heroic figure of the 'resistance to British imperialism'. Don't make me sick. It's all so bloody backward. And once again, it is so typical of men. They like going around sticking guns into people. Very phallic, isn't it?

Yeah, well, that was Uncle Paddy. Very phallic. His poor wife was never but the one way: pregnant. Well, sometimes she was suckling, but as soon as she stopped suckling, she was pregnant again. In twenty years, I was told by one of the other aunts – Eithne I think – Aunty Delia never had a period. Because she was either pregnant or breastfeeding. Uncle Paddy never left her alone – that was what I heard the aunts say. He was a man who wanted a lot of sex, and he considered that she was there to provide it.

And of course hang the consequences. She gave birth to ten children, and I believe there were miscarriages in between. Apparently, she once went to Confession and told the priest that her husband's sexual demands were insatiable. Do you know what the priest replied? 'It is your duty to submit.' Submit!

I have learned a lot about birth control during the course of my own life – I certainly went through the whole supermarket of contraception myself – and I read a book recently about how bourgeois society managed to control fertility before the advent of contraception. Of course the British were practising contraception since at least the First World War, but it was very little known in Ireland until the 1960s. Fertility was controlled, therefore, by the device of marrying late, and by abstinence. *Coitus interruptus* – probably the most widely practised form of birth control during the 19th century – was forbidden by the Church, of course, as it frustrated Nature's call to procreate.

Remembering my aunts and their contemporaries in 1940s Ireland, it was remarkable how well-controlled their fertility was. My recollection was that in middle-class society, people generally had two, three or possibly four children. The large families of ten, eleven and twelve, were distinctly working-class. Or possibly rural. And I think the reason for this is because the bourgeoisie had less sex. Uncle Matt and Aunty Flo had three children – all sons. Aunty Eithne and Uncle Gerry were childless. Aunty May remained unmarried. Because of my mother's death, we were only two. For various reasons, including restraint – in Aunty Flo's case, I imagine – there was no population explosion. But Aunty Delia and Uncle Paddy had a large family because they never stopped having sex without recourse to contraception. It was as simple as that.

Fortunately, Delia was a healthy woman, and the pregnancies didn't seem to harm her, physically. She was also of a serene turn of mind and her large family didn't cause her psychological distress either. What bugged me, when I began to understand it, was that Aunty Delia was forced to have these babies. That she hadn't chosen them. And that she had no way of stopping them or changing the situation. I remember quite well when she was in tears over the ninth baby – it must have been the tenth or eleventh pregnancy, counting the miscarriages. I overheard her tell Aunty Eithne, in the kitchen in Rathmines. 'I'm in the family way again,' she said dolefully, sighing yet kind of resigned. 'Poor Delia,' Auntie Eithne commiserated. 'How awful for you!' 'Sure there's nothing I can do about it!' Aunty Delia replied in a wobbly voice. She was miserable, poor thing.

Maybe I am just seeing it now in retrospect, but yet I seem to remember thinking, even then, when I was only about eleven, that this was a dreadful cruelty foisted on women. That you could be imprisoned, also, by a pregnancy. That there was *nothing you could do about it*. The sheer powerlessness of the situation was pitiful. Remember Simone de Beauvoir's telling phrase about the position of a pregnant woman? 'Nature's plaything.' Awful. I became extremely committed to birth control and abortion rights when I was a young woman. I've had three abortions myself. *I* was not about to respond like Aunty Delia, with that terrible, terrible female passivity, and sigh: 'Sure there's nothing I can do about it.' There bloody well was something *I* could do about it. I took control of my life, of my biological functions.

Granted, that ninth baby turned out to be my cousin Kevin, who is a brilliant guy – a top mathematician who went on to become a remarkable computer buff, and very rich, to boot – and if the announcement of his imminent entry into the world was greeted with tears, he nonetheless grew up to be the apple of his mother's eye. Poor Aunty Delia went rather senile relatively early in old age, if you know what I mean, and her children certainly were wonderful to her. The fact that there were so many of them made it easier on each of them. Sharing a dotty old lady out between ten offspring is a lot easier than sharing the burden between two. I can see, certainly that the advantage of a large family comes in old age. But I still maintain that Aunty Delia should have been able to choose the number of children she wanted. And that she should have been able to have sex without always getting pregnant.

The funny thing was that when she did become senile, Aunty Delia also became quite alarmingly frank about her sexual experiences, and it transpired that she had rather enjoyed getting it so regularly, and hugely missed it when she became a widow in her late sixties!

I'll have just one more cigarette, and maybe another dash of vodka, and then I'll go. It's getting late. But I must finally tell you about Aunty May.

Aunty May was my mother's youngest sister. She was, as I said, single. That was the problem. As the youngest daughter, it was made plain to her that she was expected to stay at home and look after her elderly parents. They did that in those days. They kept one daughter at home to care for the old folk. Barbarous, wasn't it?

In fact, her father died in the 1930s when May was still in her middle twenties. And there she was, more or less alone in the family home near Mallow, County Cork, expected to wait hand and foot on her demanding old mother. She should have told the old bag to go to hell. But then, you see, women *didn't* strike out on their own very much then because they didn't have the means. Grandmother had the moneybags, and gave May to understand that she would inherit a tidy sum if she did her duty. Which meant staying at home and not striking up any romances that might lead to marriage.

There was a man in her life, in fact. A Gordon Smart, from Cork city. I think Aunty May was probably very much in love with him, but among other obstacles he was, of course, a Protestant. And that wouldn't do. The shame of a 'mixed' marriage! I gather his folks weren't keen either and the relationship was successfully sabotaged. In the end, he joined the RAF and I believe died over Berlin in 1942. So there was Aunty May. The spinster aunt whose one sweetheart had been killed off in the war.

She was quite a gregarious woman by nature and she did try to build a social life. But she was so firmly squashed by Grandmother. May would say, for instance – 'I think I'll join the tennis club this summer.' And Grandmother would disapprove. 'I don't think that would be very interesting for you, May dear. You'll only be disappointed again.' In the end, May turned in on herself, became timid.

The one mercy of this system of daughter-looking-after-elderly-parents in days gone by was that old people then didn't live all that long. They usually kicked the bucket at a perfectly considerate age – say, their early seventies. That still gave the spinster daughter time to enjoy herself a bit. Grandmother, however, showed no such thoughtfulness. She lived on and on and on and *on*, getting deafer and more cantankerous all the time. She was within spitting distance of 90 when she finally had the grace to go, but by then May herself was in her sixties. It was far too late for her to change her life. And worse, May found herself with financial difficulties: Grandmother had not been well advised financially, after all, and things were in a muddle. May spend her last years fretting about money, being intimidated by tax inspectors who terrorize these old ladies like something out of Stalin's Russia. That was another thing: women were not properly educated to manage money. The idea was, there would always be a man to do that. In the end, she sold her house and its contents for a song. When I see *bric-à-brac* nowadays at the Kensington Antiques Fair, and notice what it fetches, I think of the treasures that poor Aunty May let go. She had some pictures by the artist Leo Whelan, which she sold for about £20 each. I saw a Leo Whelan fetch £15,000 in a Belgravia gallery. These poor women were just not permitted to develop their own judgment.

When I hear complaints nowadays about conditions in

geriatric hospitals and in residential homes for the elderly, *I* don't think: 'How dreadful that the elderly end up in geriatric wards.' I think that it is better that they should be professionally cared for than that they should ruin some young woman's life – like Aunty May's – by selfishly keeping her at home as an unpaid nursemaid.

It was yet another monstrous exploitation of women.

Now, don't you understand why I am a raging feminist, and why I have lived my life so differently? Yes, I'm still angry at what women went through. I hear the clamorous voices of women in the past – like my aunts – driven into domestic drudgery, imprisoned by authoritarian husbands, forced into endless childbearing, exploited as spinsters. I was determined to change things, to live my life differently, and I'm bloody glad that feminism became a force to be reckoned with, again, during my adulthood.

I am glad that I haven't had to suffer the sort of conditions that my poor aunts had to put up with: that I've been able to choose not to have children, not to waste my life homemaking, not to have to 'serve' society the way women were pressurized to do in the past.

Goodness – is that the time? Past midnight! I must fly. I can see you're exhausted. I shouldn't have kept you up so late. I'll ring for a taxi now. I'll just have another drink in the meantime. They say that talking about oneself at some length is a classic sign of loneliness. Another old wives' tale, if you ask me!

An Early Spring

'The choice is yours,' the doctor had said. 'Only you can make it.'

Amanda was accustomed to making choices and decisions. She was indeed a particularly effective decision-maker. Quick, shrewd, and intuitive about what would work. But for almost the first time in her life she felt, in spite of herself, a hesitancy about this decision.

For most of her life, Amanda had been spared the decisions about fertility that had so wracked her contemporaries. At the age of eighteen, she had been given surgery for a serious ovarian cyst and in the aftermath of the operation it had been revealed to her – not very tactfully – that she was unlikely ever to bear a child.

Her Fallopian tubes, the Australian surgeon had said, had been pretty well buggered up. Look on the bright side, he had added, with a grin. She could get laid whenever she liked, without having to worry too much about the consequences. Thanks, she had said glumly. I could do the same if I took the Pill. He had shrugged. Only trying to do his best, he said.

The Aussie surgeon had been robust with her; he had trod more delicately with her mother. He had explained helpfully that this was a matter of Amanda's *life*, Amanda's *health*. It was sad that she wouldn't have the choice of child-bearing, but it was better to save her life and her health now. Her mother, tormented by the fear that her teenage daughter might have cancer, nodded in agreement, if tearfully. Better to save her life and her health. Everyone couldn't have babies, and Amanda was among those, now, who wouldn't be able to.

Actually, looking back, Amanda thought the Aussie surgeon was canny in his way of tackling things. Instead of giving her a youthful complex about being infertile, he had tried to be positive about it. He was right, in his approach. Better to look on the bright side. Stop worrying about decisions over child-bearing and get on with your life. There was a lot to be said for that approach.

Being young, Amanda had accepted that decision. She had come to terms, at the age of eighteen, with the notion that she would never have children. She could plan her life, her career, without having to take into consideration the anguishing choices of so many of her contemporaries. Contraception had liberated women of her generation, but it had also presented them with this terrible question of when was the right time to have a baby.

They had looked at it every which way. There were those who concluded that it was better to have your babies young, and then start your career. Her friend Gillian Wetherby had decided on that option. So Gillian had spent her early twenties deep in nappies and childcare, while she and her husband struggled on student grants. It was hell. Hardly less hell were the life-questions presented by Caroline McNee. In an effort to resolve the conflicting demands of her fertility, Caroline had undergone no fewer than four abortions: she consoled herself that another friend of hers had had *nine* (there's always someone worse off than yourself). Angela Walker had had herself sterilized at 25 – privately, because the National Health wouldn't do it for a woman under 35 – after a series of contraceptive failures. At 30, she had met the man of her dreams and had gone through a long series of operations to have herself de-sterilized. Candida Wilson had used the Pill consistantly for twelve years, and then found it impossible to conceive, and *then* she went in for test-tube fertilization, at huge expense. Deirdre Boyd had had an IUD, and got a pelvic infection, which gave her endless trouble. Helen Smith had used the mini-Pill with success, but had to get a fertility drug to help her conceive; then she had three children in quick succession and had to get another pill to stop her conceiving.

It was hard to get contraception just right. Sure, women had choices. That was great. But Nature still found a way of playing havoc with women's lives, because the choices didn't always seem to be matched to the timing and the events.

Amanda was spared all that. She had no choice. She was told, quite simply, that she would never have a baby. And she adjusted her life to that knowledge.

All through her twenties and early thirties, this had simplified things for Amanda. She pursued her career and established it with distinction, after a couple of false starts: she enjoyed her pleasures with gusto and in moderation, and never thought twice, or even once, about her womb. She sympathized with her friends' difficulties in the battle with birth control, and rejoiced when they produced babies that they genuinely desired. She was thoroughly sane about it all. Her parents were reconciled to the fact that they would never have grandchildren because Amanda was infertile and Mike, her brother, was gay. So the family pressure was off.

When her mother died of breast cancer, Amanda was saddened by her premature death at the age of 58. But, after grieving quite appropriately, she adjusted to it with her usual common sense. When her father died in a freak road accident not very long afterwards, Amanda reflected that he had enjoyed a good life; he had become a top-level Civil Servant, a specialist in the Middle East, advising the Foreign Secretary and eventually the Prime Minister on Gulf affairs. He had had his own fulfilment. He didn't need grandchildren to validate his passage through this world. He got on well enough with his son and daughter and had reason to feel proud of what they had achieved: Amanda's public relations and marketing business was really on take-off by the time her father died, and Mike, too, had become a successful theatre costume designer. If she was honest, Amanda probably grieved a little more for her father than her mother, and possibly felt, then, the shock – which is always a shock, at whatever age – of being an orphan. But she was not neurotic about these life crises and saw them in perspective.

It was very shortly after her father's death, in fact, that the totally unexpected happened. She had gone to bed with an old colleague who had been passing through London, in that mood of half-cordiality, half-loneliness that hits busy city people every now and again. And against all medical predictions, she had become pregnant.

She had suspected something was happening when the usual symptoms of pregnancy occurred; yet discounted a pregnancy in her case. She had gone to Dr O'Brien for a consultation. He had known immediately it was a pregnancy – the old-fashioned skilled physician who can locate an embryo from the first few weeks.

'I can't be having a baby,' she told him. 'It's impossible.'

'You were unlikely to conceive,' he said. 'But it's happened just the same. Nature's drive to procreate is voracious, you know. It tries every trick in the bag to get that egg fertilized. Nature creates life where there is no life. In the desert, in droughts, in famines, Nature keeps up the pressure relentlessly.

'Starving women in concentration camps have conceived. Women dying of malnutrition in Africa have given birth. When a man penetrates a woman, millions of sperm swim upwards, trying to find an egg to fertilize. By hook or by crook, the persistent sperm gets there!

'You were very unlikely to conceive, of course. Because your Fallopian tubes were so damaged, it was a million-to-one chance that a sperm could get through. But one persistent sperm did get through! And bingo! Nature triumphed once again!

'That is Nature,' said Dr O'Brien. 'The choice thereafter is yours. We have moved away from being slaves of nature. We can choose.'

Amanda appreciated Dr O'Brien's fairness.

'I'll choose,' she said.

He shrugged. 'You must,' he responded. 'We can do a

termination. Or we can give you every support in a pregnancy. Only one thing to remember. This is the only choice you have got. It is extraordinary, in your circumstances, that you have become pregnant. You will not get this choice again. So choose wisely!' He smiled again.

It was a brilliant February day. When she left the surgery, she thought she had seldom seen the sky so blue and the air so soft and mellow, for that time of the year. Was it just an exceptionally early spring, Amanda wondered, or was it the greenhouse effect – that ecological disaster that was about to pass over the world and bring new havoc?

She passed a school playground and noticed the high-pitched sounds of childish voices at play. The dear little children! Amanda felt exhilarated at the sound, just as she felt exhilarated by nature, sunshine, even blossoms on the trees so early in the year.

She walked along the Old Brompton Road. She had taken a taxi to the surgery and had decided to walk back, for so long as it pleased her. She understood what Dr O'Brien was saying, about the vagaries of Nature, and she was not about to be hoodwinked by Nature's charms, but still, she felt exhilarated. She felt wonderful. Strong, commanding, powerful. She felt like a ship in full sail, ready to combat an armada of difficulties. It was curious that despite this inconvenience of having to break up her business day with a visit to her doctor, despite the even greater inconvenience of having to take a couple of days off the following week to accommodate the termination – it was curious that she felt suffused by this strange euphoria.

She knew what Dr O'Brien was getting at when he invoked this metaphor of Mother Nature, always at our elbow, always nudging us to procreate, procreate, procreate. She suspected that this extraordinary buoyancy and sense of well-being was just Mother Nature again, using a physical trick to persuade the mind to accept a pregnancy. She could imagine this Mother

Nature character – a big, fat, powerful creature, always coaxing and wheedling and pushing forward her interest. No, no, Amanda told herself: I must be rational. *I* am in control of my body. *I* am in control of my life. This is going to be dealt with sensibly.

Yet what she felt, in addition to the well-being, was a sense of biological triumph. Having dismissed the worry of fertility to the ditherers like Caroline McNee and their will-I-won't-I time-wasting indecisiveness, Amanda now realized that she was flattered, gratified and full of self-congratulation at the news that she could become pregnant after all. Perhaps it was only one chance in a million, but it had happened. Ah, but there's another of Nature's tricks: it is all organized so that you *should* feel gratified, it is part of her department labelled 'Motivation'. Because confirmation of fertility gratifies human beings, they go on fertilizing. What hope has contraception, a mere technology, against the machinations of Mother Nature that work in a thousand conscious and unconscious ways?

As she headed towards the Earl's Court, Amanda realized that she needed to use the loo – again. That, of course, was another classical sign of pregnancy: 'frequency of micturition'. She saw the Bolton Arms ahead of her and entered it.

It was an unattractive pub to Amanda – rough and seedy, reverberating with noisy tuneless heavy-metal music; a diffident young man in semi-punk fashions served behind the bar. Amanda decided to ask for a Perrier, in exchange for using the toilet.

Poor old Dad: poor old Mum: they would indeed have been pleased about her pregnancy, if they had lived. But then, would she have bothered to tell them, if she was going to terminate it? There seemed little point. On the other hand, if they had been alive, it was possible that they might have subtly exerted pressure to continue the pregnancy. Or perhaps one should put it in a different perspective: perhaps if you have living parents whom you get on with all right, perhaps you feel more inclined to give them a grandchild?

Amanda sipped the Perrier a little and went into the toilet. It was clean enough – as well it should be, just before lunch – yet squalid and full of aggressive graffiti. The lock on the door was broken, and 'Fuck England' was written on the door's panel. Christ, Amanda was glad to think that she would not be bringing a child into this world – a world of drugs and nihilism and alienation and anger and aggression and desperation. She went back to the bar and took her drink over to the window. She saw a mother pass by on the street, pushing a buggy which contained a child of about two, while a baby was slung in a papoose around her neck. The young mother looked pale and thoroughly harassed. Poor thing, Amanda reflected. She probably lived in a high-rise block, probably on social security, and she was as likely to be a single mum as not. Why do these young women do it? All these babies in pushchairs! It's Nature again, isn't it, insidiously persuading them that this would bring fulfilment; and all it brings is broken veins, broken sleep, broken dreams, and children screaming until you could shake them.

Of course, Amanda thought then, if I did have a child, I could hire a nanny. That would make life a lot pleasanter. She would sooner hire a day-nanny – someone who came in each day – rather than someone who slept in. She would pay her well. It is good management policy to pay well and get a highly qualified candidate. Amanda managed people well, in business, and she was sure she would be a successful employer for a nanny. But then, she wasn't going to have a child, was she? So the question didn't arise.

Amanda left the pub, and began to walk down Redcliffe Gardens towards Fulham Road. Oh, it was a perfect, perfect day; a sort of God's-in-his-heaven-all's-right-with-the-world day now that she was in the fresh air once again, away from the moral squalor of the Bolton Arms. And it was only then, really, as she began her walk back to her own flat, that she began to think about Anton.

Good heavens, Amanda reproached herself, that is an indication of how self-absorbed you have been, Amanda Spottiswoode! It would be reasonable, after all, to consider Anton, who had, when all was said and done, produced the one-in-a-million sperm that managed to swim up through her scarred Fallopian tubes and fertilize the egg. The trouble was, she wasn't sure how useful it was to tell Anton? Did he need to know? Would his reaction sway her in any way? Anyway, he was in New York now, and it's not satisfactory talking about these matters on the telephone. It wasn't, either, as though it was a serious relationship, in that sense. Their coupling had just been, so to speak, a friendly gesture. It didn't mean anything. Well, it obviously did mean something now – biologically it had created a pregnancy – but it hadn't meant anything emotionally. Mind you, she didn't object to Anton as a stud. In the genes department, his were probably as good as any, and better than most: musical, clever, Jewish, funny, not bad-looking, mildly neurotic – but who wasn't?

It would be the decent thing to inform him, however, She would write him a letter. Or ask him when he was next coming to London. Or maybe arrange a meeting in Frankfurt, or, possibly Brussels. It would be wrong to conceal it from him. Would it be right to give him an entitlement to express his opinion on the matter of the termination? It might be wrong not to. Amanda despised feminists who went around shouting about their rights without conceding the rights of others. Of course it was the case that some people argued that the foetus had rights too: a thought struck Amanda – Anton would not think like that, would he? Surely not! It was a Roman Catholic thing, not a Jewish thing, about foetuses having rights: Jews believed in the *breath* of life, that life only began when you drew breath. Still, he was the kind of man who just might turn out to be sentimental on these issues. He had been married, but had never had children because his wife hadn't wanted them. He had mentioned that this had saddened him, hadn't he? Yes, he just might lean towards having the baby. Oh well, that would just have to be faced. She would tell him fairly and squarely that it wasn't on, but she was always glad to hear his views anyway.

Amanda decided that she would go into the office that afternoon and start re-arranging schedules for next week. She would try to fix the termination for Monday, recoup on Tuesday a bit, and organize Monday's meetings for Wednesday. She had to get a new car next week too, she remembered. She had planned that and was going to a Volvo showroom in North London. A *Volvo*. Volvo had a cunning, below-the-belt advert running at the moment, showing a child's hand in the hand of an adult, obviously its parent. 'It changes your life,' said the caption, alluding to parenthood. 'Maybe it should change your car.' Mother Nature must have been rubbing her fat old hands at that line of copy! Flaunting the tenderness and care and satisfying feelings of taking responsibility for someone that parenthood brings. It wasn't just selling the Volvo: it was selling parenthood.

Of course, Amanda reflected, as she passed St Luke's church, the Volvo was indeed a car with a good safety record if one was thinking of having children. Plenty of space for a carrycot too.

But as I am not going to have any children, she lectured herself, that aspect of the car's function is irrelevant. Just be practical and realistic, and emphasize the negative, went her thoughts. Think of your cousin Helen, whose teenage children are such a heartbreak to her: one on cocaine, one so uncontrollable he beats her up, one totally rejecting of his parents. Just think of how badly people talk about their parents! Remember everyone at university: they loathed their parents. Despised their old man and scorned their potty old maters. Think of what parents suffer. Remember poor Meredith Morgan, a colleague of hers working in PR: her child had been struck down by leukaemia, and, in spite of repeated, agonizing visits to hospital and awful, frightening treatment, the little girl had died. Meredith just never got over the day when her daughter had said: 'I'm going to die, Mummy, aren't I?' How do you face a child with that pain? It is beyond endurance. Better never to risk being in that position, ever:

better to refuse life than to give it and then lose it.

In this context, Shakespeare was wrong. It was not better to have loved and lost: it was better not to have got involved at all.

And yet, in this early spring, this wonderful sunshine and brightness, this flowering, this blossoming, this air burgeoning with the earth's warm expectations, with the birdsong of mating and begetting, Amanda was suffused with that optimism that always returns to the human heart with the resurrection of growth. Life is a cycle, Amanda thought, we spring, we grow, we mature, we decay, we return to that cycle. We cannot wholly repudiate Nature, since we are organically bound up with it. As she came to the Fulham Road, she remembered the little church just on the left of the turning where dear, dear Jimmy's funeral had taken place. Death and life, all mingled, somehow. She turned the corner to see if it was open. It wasn't. You could just peer in through the porch. 'Church closed for security reasons,' it said. 'It's all stealin' nowadays,' said an old Scotswoman who was in the porch as Amanda peered in. 'People never thieved from churches in the old days. All respect is gone today! All gone!'

Amanda smiled in a kind of neutral assent and turned to go, remembering dear Jimmy's funeral, and the stunned look on his parents' face that their bright, funny, nice 26-year-old son had been killed when riding his bike, early in the morning. In fact, he was cycling back from Amanda's flat: he was a fitness fanatic. But a truck had just mown him down. Amanda had felt stunned by the bereavement – it was the first time that she had known someone of her generation to die. She had loved Jimmy, too. Yet what his parents had endured . . . who *would* be a parent? It involves too much pain, Amanda told herself. Far too much. She turned to go, and noticed a pretty piece of stained-glass work over the porch door. It was the Annunciation – which apparently Anthony Blunt had said was the most frequently-painted moment in history. The moment when the Angel tells Mary that she is with child, and the child will be Jesus. Amanda looked for a moment in wonder. She was not really a believing Christian – like many people, she wasn't sure what she was.

Yet, if this was the most painted subject in the history of European art, it must be because it meant something to people, it touched their imagination. She noticed the blue of Mary's dress, the sweet note of acceptance in her face. That was, perhaps, how men liked to think of women, in past times: forever accepting!

The church had looked in better condition for Jimmy's funeral – but then that was more than twelve years ago now. Let's see, Amanda thought: I'm thirty-four now: I was just twenty-two when that happened. Yes, just over twelve years. Doesn't time go by so quickly? Where do our lives go? *From our birthday until we die: is but the blinking of an eye.* Amanda remembered that from her Yeats period. And if life hurries by so quickly, should we leave something, or someone behind us, to mourn us? Amanda had given some passing thought, in recent years, to her ageing years, when she might well expect to be alone. She didn't think she would marry, now. She quite liked the single life. Loved her own flat, could be happy with her own company as a contrast to the very gregarious quality of her work. But when she had thought about all that, before, she had not had a choice. Now she did have the choice.

She was very, very glad, actually. Besides the satisfaction of actually having conceived – a purely biological reaction, she was convinced, over which we have little rational control – she was also glad to have the opportunity, now, to choose freely. She was glad to take a few moments out of her busy life and think about the Big Questions – life and death and nature and what things mean, or what makes us tick. A sudden pregnancy – or, Amanda corrected herself, an unexpected discovery of a pregnancy, since all pregnancies take more or less the same time to occur – brought out these philosophical questions. It was good.

She remembered there was a flower shop just along the road a little. She went in and filled her arms with blooms and greenery, yearning to be surrounded by growth and spring, and took a taxi the rest of the way back to her home in Chelsea Harbour.

She went into the office during the afternoon – took a boat up the river to Charing Cross, exulting in the breeze over the Thames – and saw her secretary Siona, who, of course, didn't fail to remark how wonderful Amanda was looking: how clear and glowing her skin. Amanda smiled cryptically. And that's another trick of Nature's, she thought. Pumps you full of hormones so you look like you've just had an Estée Lauder special.

She told Siona that she would be out of the office probably on the following Monday and Tuesday – she needed to have a wisdom tooth out. She fibbed about the abortion she was planning simply because Siona did not need to know: there was no point involving her, either.

Amanda slept very well that night, and towards morning, she was awakened by a full bladder and an urgent need to pass water. She tripped out to the bathroom, half-asleep; and relieved herself. Indeed, what a relief! Then she stumbled back to bed, and glanced at the clock: 5 a.m: another ninety minutes. She settled back on the pillow and began to drift back into a cozy, warm, doze. And then it happened – or so it seemed to her that it happened then, soon after she had glanced at the clock. There was a figure by the window, a figure in a blue cloak just like the one she had looked at in the church porch, but larger, softer, more enveloping, smiling, maternal. The figure wasn't speaking to her, but words were coming into her head that seemed to come from the figure. 'You're afraid of life, Amanda,' the words said. 'You're afraid of feeling. Don't be afraid of life and love and attachment. That's what life *is* – risking to love, risking to lose. Don't be afraid of being hurt by feelings – experience them. That is what makes you a human being.'

The figure seemed to shimmer there. I am having an apparition, Amanda thought at another level of her consciousness. I am like all those dopey shepherdesses on Bosnian hillsides. I am having an apparition of the Virgin Mary.

She suddenly opened her eyes and sat up. She turned on the bedside light. Of course there was no one there! What hallucinatory rubbish! She got out of bed, went to the kitchen and poured herself a small glass of milk and got back to bed; and slept again, tranquilly.

It wasn't, actually, until half-way through the morning that she remembered the experience. Classic case of psychological projection, she told herself. You were thinking about 'Mother Nature'; then you saw a stained-glass window, which impressed you, of the Virgin Mary. Naturally, the unconscious mind fused them together as some sort of general maternal allegorical figure. A perfectly reasonable explanation.

Yet the dream, or experience, stayed with her with a certain insistence. A reasonable explanation, yes, she told herself, but perhaps one should listen to the sub-conscious mind, just the same.

The next day Amanda phoned Dr O'Brien. 'Thanks for giving me such balanced advice yesterday,' she said. 'I think . . . I think I'll defer the decision.'

'It's not a decision that should be deferred more than three or four more weeks,' he told her. 'You would be well advised to decide before you are thirteen weeks pregnant.'

'I mean,' said Amanda, almost surprised herself. 'I mean I think we'll let nature have her way.'

'You've thought about it seriously?'

'I've thought about it very seriously. I want to have the baby. I thought, at first, it wasn't sensible, but gradually . . . some sort of instinct has come over me.'

'Yes, I know it well. It's called the maternal instinct. Okay, if that's your decision, that's fine, and if you want me to look after you during the . . . pregnancy, come back and visit me.' He smiled his goodbyes over the telephone piece, and put down the instrument. He could have seen this coming. He could have seen it coming a mile. Despite Amanda's apparent business-like approach at the start, she had given away a telling clue, a clue that usually indicates that a woman wants to continue a pregnancy. She had used the word 'baby'. Always the giveaway.

John O'Brien walked over to his surgery window and looked out at Cornwell Gardens. Good heavens, the blossoms were amazingly advanced. It certainly was an early spring. Exhilarating, life-enhancing, life-affirming: yes.

Theory and Practice

Now, before I relate this story, I would like to explain that I am the chairwoman – no, we do not say chair*person* – of the Christian Moral League. The Christian Moral League, as some people will know, is an organization which works very hard, and I might say, much against the grain these days, to uphold marriage and the family. We have our work cut out, in these times of seemingly galloping divorce, promiscuity, AIDS and abortion. We see our particular task as trying to preserve marriage, first and foremost, as that is the basis of stability and fidelity. If our marriages were more stable, well, the rest would follow, wouldn't it? You wouldn't have all this promiscuity and divorce, if you had sound marriages; and neither would you have anything like the number of abortions. We have researched many studies which show that abortion goes hand in hand, as it were, with the fragility of marriage; if people would only believe in marriage, then they would have that commitment to love and family, you see, which looks favourably on babies as the outcome of conjugal love. As it were.

No, I'm not married myself, as it happens. Let's say the right man didn't appear at the right time. There is a role in life for single people, too, you know, in family relationships. I have six nieces and nephews, and I cared for my elderly mother, bless her, for many years. I share my home, and indeed, my life, with another lady, Miss Onora Whistler, who is, like me, a schoolteacher – a very artistic and sensitive person – who completely supports me in the Christian Moral League work. We really are very happy in our own little way. We have a cat, Reginald, and a dog, Bernice – a King Charles spaniel bitch – and as we share an interest in archaeology, we usually go abroad in the summer months to visit places of cultural interest. Invariably, one of the nieces or nephews will take over our little house in Chiswick and look after the pets. Then, again, we usually have a young student or an *au pair* girl staying with us during the academic year to help us housekeep.

And that is where I come to the point at issue. One of our recent *au pairs* was a charming Scottish girl called Heather McNeil. Of course, *au pair* girls usually come from the Continent to learn English, but, in this case, Heather answered our advertisement and we took her. She was doing a catering course in London and needed accommodation in exchange for housekeeping help and some pocket money, and she was one of the nicest young people we have had in our home. She stayed the usual academic year – from September until late June – and then departed for Canada, as she was engaged to a Canadian. Like almost all of our girls (we won't say anything about the wild Scandinavian who took drugs or the difficult German who had so many boyfriends, *despite* my best endeavours *and* all the pamphlets from the Christian Moral League), Heather remained on very good terms with us and wrote us postcards from Montreal. She seemed to get on very well in Canada, and had secured an excellent job in a French-Canadian hotel and restaurant, and – this made Miss Whistler and me most happy – seemed to have made a real success of her marriage. No babies as yet, but clearly such a good girl, with such a devoted attitude to her husband. None of this horrid feminist approach about 'rights'. Believe me, when 'rights' come in the door, 'devotion' goes out the window! Marriage depends on love and self-sacrifice, not 'rights'.

So when I got a telephone call one evening – funny, I was just going out the door to a committee meeting of the CML – from a Mrs McNeil, well, it rang a bell, so to speak! It was a *very* soft voice, that soft, feminine, Highland Scots. 'You don't know me, Miss Wallace,' the voice said, 'but I am Heather's mother. Heather McNeil, that is.' 'Oh yes,' I said. 'Oh yes, of course, we remember Heather with great affection. I do hope everything is well with her.' 'Yes, indeed,' said the voice, a little hesitantly. 'She is very happy. And very well. She . . . she spoke so kindly about you, Miss Wallace, and how kind you and Miss Whistler had been to her. You made her stay in London a . . . home from home.'

I remembered then, that Heather had perhaps needed the home life we had been able to give her. She came from a good family, a most respectable family, but she had let us know, little by little, that not everything was as it might be in her own home. They were good, Christian people, to be sure – living in a pleasant suburb of Glasgow, though I remembered she said her mother was from one of the remoter islands. But all had not been well in that household. You see, marriage problems arise even in the best-regulated lives! We know this only too well in the Christian Moral League, oh, yes!

After a little pause, Heather's mother went on. 'Well, you see, Miss Wallace, I am visiting London, and I wonder if it would be possible to come and visit you?'

'Of course, Mrs McNeil,' I replied. Does not St Paul tell us that we must give hospitality? 'What about Tuesday week, for tea?' I said.

There was another little pause. Mrs McNeil said, in a small voice: 'Well, I wondered if I could come and see you perhaps a little sooner? I mean, perhaps, tomorrow?'

I quickly looked at the wall diary that is next to our telephone. The following day, there was a Parent-Teacher Action Committee meeting at the school. The day after, Miss Whistler and I were due to attend the annual conference for a Free Lithuania – we are both involved in Christian, anti-Communist organizations to give support to the Baltic States. Then came the weekend, with a church harvest festival and a bell-ringing competition. Our calender is, alas, very full! Still, there was something urgent in Mrs McNeil's soft tone, and I decided that people come before committees and the Parent-Teacher Action Group would just have to wait. 'Do come over tomorrow, Mrs McNeil,' I told her. 'Come for a late tea at five o'clock.'

She then asked if she could make it a teeny bit later, and I agreed. I suppose if I am to be entirely honest, the Parent-Teacher Action Committee is rather a chore, and I wasn't entirely displeased to tell my conscience that a plea of human help was more important.

Mrs McNeil duly arrived, *chez nous*, nearer six o'clock than five. She was a comely, plump woman – very pretty in a fluffy sort of way, with brown hair and brown eyes. She brought a gift of flowers – two generous bunches of chrysanthemums, which, although they remind me of the graveyards of France (Miss Whistler and I have done the tragic tour of the war graves there), are nevertheless rich in colour and scent. I made her welcome and offered her a drink. Onora was not present as she had a choir practice at the time.

I offered Mrs McNeil a drink of sparkling elderberry cocktail – a special recipe I had picked up at a Moral Re-Armament Meeting, of natural elderberry juice plus sparkling water and a touch of honey, a most wonderful combination – but Mrs McNeil rather surprised me by requesting a gin and tonic. Miss Whistler and I don't take alcoholic drink, usually, though we keep some in the pantry for emergencies, and I was able to comply with her rather bald, albeit politely made, request.

'Thank you,' she said, very gratefully. And after a couple of swallows and the usual pleasantries about admiring our garden (which is very pretty, I must admit), Mrs McNeil came very much to the point.

'I hope you will forgive me for phoning you,' she said. 'But you see, I don't know anyone, really, in London. And the truth is, I am here because I have left my husband.'

I must admit I was *very* startled. 'Left your husband?' I said.

She nodded her head, and opened her handbag. She looked

confused for a moment and took out a cigarette. I had to dive into the kitchen to find an ashtray, as we do not often have guests who smoke. However, as my dear mother used to say (she took a puff herself, actually), *chacun à son goût*!

'I'm sorry to hear that,' I said to Mrs McNeil sympathetically. I wasn't merely *sorry* to hear it – I was appalled. From what Heather had told me, there were five children in this family.

'Yes,' said Mrs McNeil, who had told me that her name was Betty. 'I've stood it for so long, Miss Wallace, and I just can't stand it any more! I found him with his latest young woman, *in . . . fla . . .*'

'*In flagrante delicto?*' I prompted.

'Yes.' She took a handkerchief from her handbag, which was, I noticed, much-worn and of imitation leather. 'Yes. In a very compromising position indeed.'

'Dear, dear,' I said, not quite knowing what else to say.

'Of course, he's always had other lady friends,' Betty McNeil went on. 'Almost since we were first married. But recently, it's got out of hand completely. And he's been more and more cruel to me. He's kept me a sort of prisoner. He's put a lock on the telephone. When I took a small, part-time job in a craft shop in Glasgow, he rang up and said I was an alcoholic and that I shouldn't be employed. When I found another job, he passed me every morning at the bus-stop, while he drove into town in the Rover. Worst of all,' she became very tearful, 'he won't speak to me.'

'Oh dear,' I said again. Then mindful of the Christian Moral League's main concern I said: 'What about the children, Mrs McNeil?'

She blew her nose.

'The children urged me to leave him,' she said. She fumbled in the cheap bag again. She drew out a crumpled letter. 'This is from Heather,' she said. She handed it to me.

It was, indeed. I glanced through it. I saw Heather's writing, underscored with concern. 'You *must* get away from this monster,' Heather wrote to her mother. 'Just *go*. Take what money you have and go.'

Betty McNeil referred to this point in the letter immediately. 'I had a small dowry,' she said. 'My family set up a small deposit account – well, about seven thousand pounds – for me, when I married Rory. It was in case I ever needed it. I used some of it for various necessities over the years, but some of the capital is still on deposit. I used it to run away.' And she bit her lip as she confessed this.

Well! As you can imagine, I was still flabbergasted. While I thought about my response I went away and got some more gin and tonic. Lucky we had those emergency supplies!

As I was fetching Mrs McNeil another drink, my thoughts were in a whirl. It was clear to me where my duty lay. It was to tell Mrs McNeil to return to her husband forthwith. I decided to ask her about her other children, as I returned to the living-room.

'Well,' she said, in response. 'My son is away to sea, in the Navy, so he's all right. Then the next girl, after Heather, is at university – in Durham. She's clever, doing modern languages. There are just two left at home, a boy and a girl. They seem to be able to cope with my husband. The girl is still at school, the boy is on a training course. They both said I should go. My son said he couldn't bear to see me insulted any more.'

'I see,' I pondered. If all the *children* thought that the mother should leave the father – this seemed pretty strong evidence.

'And how are you managing in London?' I asked. 'It must be expensive for you, being here.'

She nodded. 'It is.' She had found digs, she said, in Cricklewood. It was a modest room, a long way from the tube, and it cost £50 a week. It hadn't been easy. She had trudged around with her two suitcases, initially paying £38 a night in a down-at-heel hotel in Bloomsbury. She had found temporary work as an office filing clerk. She was fifty, she said, but she had been trained as a secretary and was still able to do everyday office work.

'Does your husband miss you?' I asked. Surely the husband must see the error of his ways!

She shook her head. 'I think that he doesn't miss me at all. My younger daughter tells me that he is having a grand life for himself now, with his fancy lady.'

Our front door opened and it was Onora. She came in, fresh-faced. 'This is Betty McNeil,' I said, meaningfully. Onora rose to the occasion. 'Hello, Betty,' she replied. 'I have three delicious *wiener schnizels* here from our Polish delicatessen and we shall have supper immediately. Do join us.' Onora is very good at making people feel welcome. Prescient, too, with provisions.

Onora cooked supper while Betty McNeil and I talk further about her dilemma. It was clear that she really did not know what to do, that she was looking for a home from home.

'Perhaps,' she said tentatively, 'if you don't have a housekeeper at the moment, I could stay here, and be your housekeeper.'

As it happened, we didn't have anyone at that point, though we had agreed to take on a Polish girl in three weeks' time. Yet I did not like the idea of aiding and abetting an absconding wife to run away from her marriage. I had to speak the truth.

'I don't think you are doing the right thing,' I told Betty. 'I think you should sort out your marriage. You can't just leave your children behind. What would become of the world if all mothers ran away?'

She didn't have anything to say to this.

'And you must have loved your husband once,' I went on.

She thought. 'Yes,' she said. 'I did. I thought he was a thoughtful man, because he wasn't talkative. Then he became ever so silent, awkward, irritable. I thought he was decisive. Then he became bossy and intolerant. I thought he was understanding of the women he worked with. Then I learned that he slept with them.'

Then she said the most devastating thing of all, I thought. 'In twenty-eight years, he has never asked me *once* how I felt about anything. He has never, ever considered my feelings, or asked my advice, or spoken to me just as a fellow human being.'

We had supper, which Onora prepared very nicely – she even brought out a pleasant bottle of Austrian wine which we keep for special occasions. Betty relaxed and seemed to enjoy it. She laughed at some of the stories that Onora told about the characters at her choir practice. She told us, too, that she liked being in London, really. The young people whom she worked with were extremely nice to her, she said. They joked with her and treated her as an individual. They made jokes about Scotland and called her Mac. She found it rather jolly.

As I was making the coffee in the kitchen – I always make proper coffee from real beans; I deplore instant coffee as I deplore instant morality – I thought about Betty's plight and how much I should help her. I hadn't heard her husband's version of the story, and yet, I thought, it must have taken a great deal of courage for this woman to have cut adrift after twenty-eight years of marriage. The children seemed to be entirely on her side. My principles about upholding marriage were, I realized, entirely at war with my sympathy for this rather brave lady.

We had coffee. I told her that I would drive her back to her bedsit in Cricklewood. I told her that I was glad to see her and that she must regard me as a friend.

Cricklewood is a spread-out part of north-west London. NW10, as I remembered from my driving-instructor – who used to take me there twenty years ago – is London's biggest geographical postal district. Street followed street, avenue followed avenue, and we finally got to Betty's bedsit. It was a tiny room in an ill-lit suburban street. The house, she told me, contained two Irishmen, two Greeks, a Moroccan and herself. She showed me her room. It was pathetic. A small suburban room, which she had pitifully tried to make personal with pictures of her children, two soft toys on the bed, and underneath the ageing dressing-table, six pairs of pretty shoes.

Shoes were obviously her weakness.

When I saw Betty's room, I weakened from all my principles. 'Betty,' I said. 'If you want to come and stay with us for a while, you're welcome.' There was something so pathetic about this bare little room! This woman had left behind a fine suburban home, for this bleakness.

'Thanks,' she said. 'That's all I want to know.' And she looked at me with great sweetness. 'It is just so wonderful to know that one has a friend,' she said, her voice trembling.

'Actually,' she added then, 'I *may* go back to my husband, or I may go and join Heather in Canada, as soon as I know the younger ones are all right. But in coming to London, in talking to you, I've just gained such self-confidence. I don't have to be rubbish under a man's feet. I've gained a certain amount of self-respect again and a feeling of freedom, and choice. It's funny: now I know I *can* break free, because I've done it.'

As I drove back to Chiswick I thought how hard it is to fit human beings to rules and regulations. It's all very well upholding the principles of marriage and the family – which I do – but sometimes you come across cases which test all those principles. It is a fact that some women – and maybe some men – are better being out of a tyrannical marriage. And sometimes these individuals are very brave in making that bid for freedom. Betty McNeil in her humble little bedsitter was a triumph of human self-reliance. All she needed was a friend, someone who would tell her that they would help her, if she needed further help.

Of course, none of this changes the principle in question. In general, I still do everything I can to support marriage and the family, to oppose easy divorce. But there *are* exceptions. Certainly there are exceptions. Then of course, they say exceptions only really prove the rule, don't they? Or do they?

The Charm of Gerry Anderson

Opinion was divided as to why Gerry Anderson had such an agreeable effect on women. He was one of those men who just always got his own way where the female sex was concerned. Women liked him, fell for him, were kind to him and climbed willingly into bed with him.

Nobody claimed that his success in this sphere was due to his appearance. He was a small, slight man with a pock-marked complexion and startling red hair. It was speculated that he must have been 'great in bed,' although what exactly this means no one is ever *quite* able to explain. It might have been his faint air of helplessness and self-neglect, which bordered on the studied – there was always a button missing, there was always a grubby anorak into which a careless pen had bled a stain. Gerry also retained the touching student's habit of rolling his own cigarettes, which gave him an added touch of vulnerability, of quaint frugality.

Thus, some believed (with some justification) that it was Gerry's bohemian disarray which so helped him to score. Never underestimate a woman's maternal instinct, observers would comment. A man who so obviously needs to be looked after will never be without a woman to look after him.

Others, of course, thought that Gerry's political reputation probably made him seem glamorous. There was some substance in this theory, too. He had led a rather exciting life during the golden years of the 1960s and 70s. He had been active at Belfast university in the middle sixties, where a lively students' Civil Rights campaign had preceded the Troubles in Northern Ireland. He had been present at the anti-Vietnam demonstrations in New York in May 1967 and at Grosvenor Square, where he had worked with Tariq Ali.

He had known Daniel Cohn-Bendit during the student *evènements* of Paris, May 1968, when all intelligent young people had believed that capitalism was finally coming to an end. Gerry had met Fidel Castro; he had carried messages from Regis Debray in a Colombian prison. In 1973, he had been one of the leading figures in a Marxist march on Rome when Salvador Allende had fallen.

All this was fearfully exciting, and brought Gerry a rich background in radical politics. It also qualified him as an honorary feminist, since revolutionaries counted as feminists until at least the late 1970s, and the rise of Thatcherism split the Left. Anyway, Gerry's political background gave him a fascinating line in conversation, and his proletarian edge was especially efficacious in the seduction of nicely-brought-up girls, thoroughly bored with the security of bourgeois life, and keen to vex their parents in Carshalton.

In truth, a large element in Gerry's appeal to women was that he was funny and incorrigibly good-tempered. 'He *always* makes you laugh,' women with experience of Gerry would explain. 'He is, in that most old-fashioned sense of the word, *gay*: droll, jolly, devil-may-care.' This indeed probably was the kernel of Gerry's charm. Despite the high-flown, serious political talk which marked much of his conversation, despite the sometimes extraordinarily dismissive statements he could make about whole sections of humanity (Allende, he claimed, would have survived if he had just put his mind to shooting the middle-classes), Gerry had a genuinely benign personality. He considered it his responsibility to entertain a woman when he was with her – in contrast to the run of men who keep their best jokes for the benefit of the pub or the club, and seldom show much real curiosity about women as people.

And thus it was that by the time he had reached thirty, Gerry

126

Anderson might easily have boasted that he did not know what it was to suffer in love, that he had never been seriously rebuffed, and that it was very seldom indeed that a woman disobliged him in any particular. He might have boasted that, but to add to Gerry's charm, he was not vulgar, and wouldn't dream of boasting about his conquests.

But then, he did not need to. His reputation did the boasting.

'Any sign of you getting married, Gerard, dear?' his mother would ask, sometimes half-ironically, yet with a perceptible note of anxiety, when he returned home to visit his parents. Although he made much of the proletarian terraced house in a slum quarter of Belfast which he pictured as his birth-place, his parents now dwelled in a pleasant suburb, being entirely respectable schoolteachers.

'Ach, sure, who'd have me?' Gerry would reply, mockingly.

'Well, now, as they used to say in the West,' – Gerry's mother came from County Galway, on the West coast of Ireland – 'it's time you were casting your eye around. You'd make some young woman a fine husband, if you'd jut put your mind to it. Especially now you've got a pensionable job!'

'Don't you know I don't hold with marriage, Mother, dear,' Gerry would banter, pouring himself tea from the big brown betty that stood on the stove, old-style. 'An outdated bourgeois institution – didn't I tell you that before!' He was always outspoken about his views with his parents, who were surprisingly easy-going, but he kept the tone jokey and light just the same. 'And who,' he went on waggishly, with a music-hall routine, 'wants to live in an institution! I say, I say, I say!'

At this point his sister Genevieve entered the kitchen, rolling her eyes. 'Your jokes should have a preservation order on them, Gerry Anderson!' Genevieve was perhaps the one woman not vulnerable to his charm; she was a superior young lady and thought him corny.

127

'That's all fine and dandy now,' his mother went on, not wanting to lose the point of the conversation. 'But one of these fine days, you might want to settle down. You might want children for yourself, in the heel of the hunt.'

Gerry understood that it was his mother who wanted the children. His elder brother was a priest in the Philippines and the youngest boy – much adored by the family – was Down's Syndrome, and would never have any progeny.

Thus Nora Anderson's chances of having grandchildren had been reduced by fifty per cent already. Only Genevieve – who was choosy and supercilious when it came to suitors – and himself could provide the next generation of babies in the family.

Gerry did not admire his parents' simple dynastic ambitions – to have grandchildren – but he was considerate about them. He had, after all, applied his political analysis very thoroughly to this subject. Having children was a means of expression for powerless people, people who had been denied personal fulfilment themselves (as he would explain to his sociology class at the Polytechnic). Having children was a form of compensation when people lacked the means of control over production and social ownership of resources. Poor people, in particular, had children to console themselves for the lack of political power in their lives. Men forced women into child-bearing to create social control, since women as mothers were more dependent on men, or society, for support. Once men – people, indeed – recognized that there were other areas of useful fulfilment, these dynastic imperatives would dissolve.

He, Gerry, did not need to disseminate his sperm pro-creatively; he could disseminate his *ideas*. That was his act of creation.

Not that Gerry considered his parents stupid. No, in their own way they were quite cultivated. But they were formed by old and reactionary ideas about the family, and not least, by the Church. Gerry had discarded all that. He was too kind to be hurtful to his mother, so he always kept the discussion on a generalized plane. And cheerful.

'Ach, well,' his mother sighed, stoking the fire. 'God is good.'

'If *She* exists,' Gerry added the feminist coda. And before his mother could throw something at him, he went on – 'I'm away to the pub. Would you like a dram?'

And so she softened, and accompanied him for a short while. Gerry was as much a gentleman when out with his mother as with any other female.

In fact, by the late 1970s, Gerry had, to all intents and purposes, quite 'settled down', though he was not married. He was living with Brita Jensen, a serious-minded Swede who had reasons – apart from being Swedish, that is – to require cheering up. Brita had left her husband and two children in Malmö on an impulse that occurs to more women than we might imagine. She felt imprisoned by being a wife and mother. It was, she often explained at the Women's Therapy Centre which she organized in Colchester – the East Anglian town where she and Gerry were, for the moment, settled – either suicide or flight. She had chosen to leave her family because marriage was literally driving her mad.

Brita had come to England to think her life out for a while, and to follow a course in Women's Studies. This led to her starting up the Therapy Centre, which was extremely busy, attracting scores of women suffering from unhappy experiences, difficult conflicts, bad marriages, problems with motherhood, problems with lack of motherhood, menstruation, menopause, abortion, miscarriage, disappointment with relationships. All the slings and arrows of the human condition – and particularly the female condition – were featured in the therapy sessions, which would sometimes seem like an endless tale of woe.

Yet Brita was gratified by the feeling that she was answering a certain need at the Therapy Centre. As time went by, she felt progressively more confident about the decision to leave her husband, but progressively more mournful about her children.

At first, she tried to be firm with herself. She was a dedicated follower of Simone de Beauvoir, and de Beauvoir had taught that 'one is not born a woman, one becomes one.' Therefore, all these things, like the so-called maternal instinct, were a matter of social conditioning. As she had never known anyone to criticize Simone de Beauvoir, there was nobody to point out to Brita that the great mistress of French letters had decidedly not been a mother herself. Brita's passionate dislike of bourgeois society was somewhat rooted in the pain of her own loss. She was thus an energetic source of assistance to other women who had known both pain and loss.

'Next time you are going to Ireland, I would like to go with you,' Brita told Gerry over a yoghurt and muesli breakfast in their minimalist white kitchen, the day after he returned from one of his visits. Brita was eating yoghurt and muesli, that is. Gerry was feeding on his ancestral fare – bacon, eggs and black pudding. 'Your family sounds nice,' she said, a little wistfully. 'I am not afraid of the bombs.'

'You're more at risk riding a bicycle here, kiddo,' Gerry said. 'Of course you should come on over the next time I'm going. You'd love it.' Actually, he wondered about that. Ireland wasn't serious enough for Brita. 'By the way,' he went on, 'talking of bikes, do you want to take the car or the bike today? You choose!'

Brita always chose the bike because she knew Gerry liked to have the car, the sturdy yellow Deux Chevaux, with its anti-nuclear stickers. She liked making the little sacrifice for him, though of course she would never have let on, because that would have sounded so unfeminist.'

'I like to take the bike, you know that,' she smiled.

Gerry went to the local poly most days, where he taught sociology. His students adored him. But his schedule allowed him absences too – nowadays mostly in connection with radio and television work in London and Bristol, rather than in demos and student riots. He *was* settling down, you see. A regular life was not at all disagreeable to him, now, and, as his mother had pointed out, the job did carry a steady pension.

For all her commitment to radicalism, Brita was accomplished in the domestic arts. She had an innate feeling for cooking, ran their home with efficiency and grace, and was a superb needlewoman. When agitated, she knitted with a marked ferocity.

One evening Gerry came home to find her knitting very furiously indeed, weaving anger into a complicated cable stitch.

'Hello kiddo,' he said, bending down to kiss her warmly. 'Trouble at the mill?'

She concentrated hard through her granny glasses. 'The Catholics are on the warpath again. They will never give up trying to turn back the clock. We must fight them. It's this Polish Pope, you know, such a disaster!'

Gerry sat down next to her, and took her hand. That was another thing about Gerry. He was soothing, consoling.

'Don't take it pessimistically, Brita. Talk to me about it.'

Brita indicated the *Guardian* lying on the glass and steel coffee table. 'It's all in the paper. There is a Private Member's bill being introduced to try to restrict the abortion law, and the Catholics are rallying all their supporters. It's *terrible*.' She went on knitting hard. She was very upset. Anything to do with babies upset her, Gerry noticed. 'Women will be forced into bad pregnancies all over again, driven back into the Bronze Age of *Kinder, Küche, Kirche*. They just want to stop women making their choices, having their freedom.'

'I'd have thought,' Gerry said cheerfully, consolingly, 'that the Bronze Age was a little too advanced for the Vatican. I'm sure they'd developed contraceptives by then – they made them out of cattle dung, remember? No, the Stone Age would suit our Polish Pope better!' He moved to the fridge and extracted two Stella Artois beers. He gave one to Brita, and sat down next to her again, putting his arm around her comfortingly. He knew that Brita was distressed about something deeper than a parliamentary bill, but then he had read his feminist tracts correctly – in addition to having good instincts, that is. 'The political is personal: the personal is political.' Here, the political certainly was personal.

'Listen,' he said to her. 'They haven't a hope in hell. Change the abortion law? Never!'

'Do you really think not, Gerry?' she looked up at him for reassurance.

'Not at all. Not a chance. Sure they're all first-class hypocrites, all that so-called Moral Majority crowd. Those respectable suburban matrons are the first to avail themselves of abortion facilities when it suits them,' he told her, as though he knew whereof he spoke, although in truth he had been extremely lucky in this department: he had never been faced with a real-life unwanted pregnancy, as it happened.

'Perhaps you are sentimental, in your heart, still, about the subject of abortion,' Brita reflected, as they were having their drinks, and Gerry was rolling a cigarette. 'Because you were brought up as a Catholic, after all.'

Gerry waved away the thought grandly. 'A cultural Catholic, kiddo. That's to do with tribal identity in Ireland; it has nothing to do with moral theology. I was reared to beat up Protestants on the way home from school, but I don't beat you up, do I, you dear little Lutheran vixen, you!'

Brita giggled. 'Oh Gerry! You are funny.' Then she said, more seriously, 'You will help our women's group against this bill, won't you?'

Gerry felt his political blood stirring. Help? The thought of a fresh political campaign was positively exhilarating. Organising, speaking, demonstrating, lobbying, using the media . . . terrific!

He took her hand and kissed it, cavalier-style. 'I'll do everything I can for you – now and always!' he said, and Brita realised, not for the first time, how much his puckered carroty face meant to her.

Gerry was as good as his word. He threw himself into the campaign to stop the 1979 abortion reform bill, activating all his connections on the Left and in the trade unions – which had previously been shy on women's issues, and especially on this somewhat delicate one. Soon he was seen carrying a banner in a

132

men's auxiliary group supporting a 20,000-strong march to Parliament, led by a well-known television personality and sex counsellor, Anna Kuttner, who happened to be heavily pregnant at the time.

The pro-choice demo pleased Gerry enormously. It had all the verve of the old Vietnam and Civil Rights marches of the sixties, yet with none of the real aggression or trouble with the police. It was marvellous to be out marching for a cause again. The demo figured on all the TV news bulletins, and he knew, by the end of the evening, that it was an unqualified success.

'Brilliant,' he pronounced, as a group from the march were relaxing in the spacious Maida Vale flat of one of the organizers. 'Take it from an old campaigner, sugar,' he told Brita. 'It was great stuff. And having a pregnant woman in the lead was the best stroke of all. What a coup!'

'It must have been jolly hard for her to do that,' remarked Louisa Eliot, pouring him a glass of Saumur. Louisa owned the flat and was being a generous hostess to over forty people that evening.

'Ach, she's very committed,' Gerry said. 'When you're committed to a cause, you shouldn't let sentimentality interfere with the political action. I quote the old slogan – 'can't make an omelette without breaking eggs'.

It was not, in the circumstances, a happy metaphor, embryos and foetuses being regarded as merely fertilized eggs by those who chose to view them as such.

Brita seemed melancholy again. 'Post-demo *tristesse*,' he murmured, stroking the back of her neck, which she liked. 'There's always a let-down after the adrenalin flows,' he explained.

'Like post-natal depression,' she added. 'After all the shoving and pushing, you become, well, flat.'

Someone passed around a joint of marijuana, and the evening ended on a calm, serene note. Brita was fine, Gerry noticed, as they were leaving. But Gerry also noticed Louisa's long, long legs, pre-Raphaelite hair and full, low-slung bosom.

A week later, Louisa of the pre-Raphaelite hair telephoned Gerry to ask him if he would like to contribute an article to the feminist magazine she co-edited.

'We don't usually feature articles by men,' she said. Louisa spoke as though she carried a small but rather hot potato in her mouth. 'The editorial collective generally gives male contributors the thumbs down, but in this case, I *think* they might see their way to making an exception.'

Gerry felt very gratified. He always felt gratified when people liked him. He was especially glad he had pleased the Stalinist-faced feminists of the Red Rag collective.

'That's a great honour, Louisa,' he said. He had that Ulster characteristic of using a person's first name easily, lightly, naturally.

'Your supportive actions on the abortion campaign were greatly appreciated,' Louisa said. 'Roz, who's strong on ideology, said that you and Peter Huntingford were the only two exceptions to the rule of general male oppression.' Peter Huntingford was an obstetrician who had also made a strong stand on abortion rights. Gerry knew Huntingford was big with the feminists and felt greatly flattered.

'Thank you very much, Louisa. Of course, I'd be delighted to write anything you'd like for the magazine.' Gerry knew that Red Rag's fees were negligible, but it would certainly help his profile as a radical. Then he went on to make the most natural suggestion in the world. 'Let's meet and have a drink and talk about it.'

'Well, I thought we could outline the details over the phone. We need 1,500 to 2,000 words on the theme of men's impulse to control women and how that has to be changed. I would leave it to you how you might want to approach it.'

'Sure, Louisa, but in my experience,' Gerry said reasonably, 'briefings of any kind work better face to face. I'd like to talk through it a wee bit more.'

'Okay.' She sounded a little reluctant, as though he were wasting her time.

It happened that Gerry was due to be in London on the

Thursday of that week, for a recording of the BBC programme *Value Judgements*, which he presented once a month. They arranged to meet, after the recording. He suggested a pub near St Martin's Lane which, unusually for London establishments, actually served some decent wine.

It was summer. The day was close and balmy, peopled with relaxing office workers.

Gerry turned up wearing a long flowery shirt from his hippy days. He looked absurd, which is often a good thing, since looking absurd is akin to looking vulnerable. We are often moved to pity by the clown.

Louisa was waiting for him. As he joined her on one of the outdoor wooden seats, she could scarcely suppress a smile. He felt cheerful. Things always went well with him when women smiled.

'Now, business before pleasure,' she drawled, as he brought her a cool glass of Chablis.

'Why the Puritan work ethic, Louisa? Why not pleasure before business?' he bantered.

'How did the programme go?' she asked, not to be cajoled.

'Fine, fine. It's funny having a Conservative administration, of course: It puts the Left culturally, as well as politically, in opposition. But Margaret Thatcher won't last long.' He took a packet of Rizla papers from his pocket and began to roll a cigarette. 'The strange thing is, you know, I could fancy her. But then I've always warmed to bossy women.'

Louisa was watching him. Her lips were parted slightly and he thought he distinguished a glint in her eye.

'That's frivolous, Gerry. Let's talk about the piece you're going to write.'

They had a short conversation about the direction of the piece. It wasn't complicated. Gerry knew what Red Rag wanted and he believed it was polite to give any woman what she wanted. Gerry's support for feminism was, in fact, a form of gallantry – not an unusual inclination in well-brought-up men. We must remember that support for the Equal Rights Amendment in America came from men who wanted to 'let the ladies have what they're asking for': opposition came from older women who knew that equality had its disadvantages.

Louisa and Gerry on their second glass of Chablis, began to talk about Ireland. She was astonished to learn that he did not support the 'armed struggle' of Sinn Fein. No, he told her, nationalism is reactionary. The true Left position should be anti-nationalist, anti-sectarian: solidarity with all the working class, Protestant and Catholic. In fact, he explained, the Protestants in Northern Ireland had a stronger tradition of true socialism than the Catholics. It was Catholicism that was feudal. It was Presbyterianism which was actually *republican*, if you subjected it to a proper political analysis.

Louisa listened with interest. She began to like Gerry. He was funny-looking, but he had something to say. His political conversation was peppered with human interest and anecdote. He was sensible, considerate, funny. And he seemed ready to please. She needed a man who would go out of his way to please her.

It is notorious that while women notice conversation and personality in a man, men first notice looks and physical responses in a woman. Gerry observed Louisa's fine green eyes, rich hair, the plainly-tailored frock which fitted at the bodice, showing her shapely bosom to advantage, her long haunches and legs. The thought flitted over Gerry's mind that he would not object to carrying her off to Regent's Park there and then, but he dismissed this sign of the crude unconscious Id as that of an escaped male chauvinist who had to be caught and handcuffed.

They parted at Leicester Square tube station, but Gerry knew he would meet Louisa again. For one thing, he had promised to deliver the article the following Thursday, when he had more business in London. It's always better to deliver an article personally, he had explained. Editorial relations are always improved by human contact, he said.

When he got back to Colchester, however, he found Brita in a distraught state, packing her bags.

She had received a call from her ex-husband, telling her that their youngest child, a boy of ten, had contracted meningitis.

'I must go to him,' Brita cried, quite overwrought.

'Ach, hush,' said Gerry, tenderly. 'Sure kids get over these things quite easily nowadays.'

'No, I must, I must . . .' Brita was beside herself. 'It is my fault, not being there. He will die. It is very bad. Oh, very *bad*, Gerry!'

Gerry felt for her. She seemed so slight and helpless, now, like a child herself. Her little granny glasses made her look like an owl-eyed schoolgirl. He wrapped his arms around her and held her very close.

Then he got on the telephone. He somehow arranged a seat on a flight to Copenhagen – the nearest convenient airport – on the following morning.

He helped her to pack while she wept incessantly. He reassured her that everything would be all right when she reached her son, that everything would be okay in Colchester while she was away, that her American assistant would take over the Therapy Centre. They went to bed and he cradled her in his arms with loving sweetness.

They rose at six the next morning and he drove her to London Airport.

Brita did not return to England for a long time. Her son died – the first case in what was to be a tragic revival of childhood meningitis. She was devastated and stayed on in Sweden with her daughter, entering a complicated legal battle for the little girl's custody. The family court eventually awarded shared custody, and Brita went to live in Lilla Edet, a quiet fishing spot on the western seaboard. She took up designing knitwear and eventually settled down there with a local artist.

Brita never forgot Gerry, and wrote to him every year, around the time of her son's death. Sadly, though, she would always associate England, and her time with Gerry, with that tragedy.

In the meantime, Gerry went on living in Colchester, teaching at the Polytechnic, and pursuing his various other broadcasting and writing activities. The tasteful minimalist flat deteriorated somewhat into Irish bachelor chaos. There was no shortage of women who wanted to share their life with Gerry, and indeed – *pace* the rules of feminism – look after him and run his household, but the truth was that being well into his thirties now, he was getting choosy.

When in London, he often saw Louisa, though it took some time for their relationship to come to fruition.

Louisa was, in some ways, a very cool customer. Her parents – now retired to Hampshire – had spent their lives in various outposts of the former British Empire. She had been born in Pakistan, lived in India, Kenya, Jamaica. She had, outwardly, the natural command of a memsahib.

She had been married, briefly, to a Yugoslav whom she described as a brute. She had lived in America for a while. She had worked on a feminist magazine in Canada and had returned to London to start up *Red Rag* with her own financial resources.

Although the magazine operated on a shoe-string, paid its contributors peanuts and was constantly stymied by the delays occasioned by collective decision-making, *Red Rag* was actually something of a success. The mainstream magazines tended to follow up stories that first appeared in it, and thanks to Jo, who ran its advertising, its revenue from small ads and display ads grew by the month.

One Thursday evening, Gerry and Louisa had dinner together in a Regents Park restaurant. She had been understanding about Brita, whom Gerry still missed rather a lot. Afterwards, she took a cab back to the Maida Vale flat and he came inside with her as though it was expected of him, as, indeed, it was.

When the flat door closed behind them, he placed a hand lightly on her sex, and looked at her with genuine desire.

'Can I?' he asked, caressing her. Now he touched her breast.

'Will you do what I want you to?' she asked, the green eyes now vividly glinting.

'Anything,' he kissed her. 'Anything.'

She responded to the kiss. 'Hurt me,' she said. 'Bruise me. Give it to me with pain.'

And so Gerry took Louisa and did as she wished, which was not entirely to his taste, but which was not entirely repugnant either, after a while. Sadists are born, not made, but all inclinations can be cultivated a little. If Louisa wanted to be beaten and bruised, if she liked to indulge in rape fantasies, well, that was her choice. It seemed a funny choice, of course, for a woman who ran campaigns against male violence and published articles which denounced men's raping instincts, but Gerry had lived long enough to understand that there was no accounting for tastes, and those who are strongest in theory are quite often weakest in practice. He was aware the he practised his own little hypocrisies – he was beginning to doubt how much he really rejected bourgeois capitalism – and that made him tolerant. He obliged Louisa: again: and again: and once again.

Gerry's article on men's traditions of social control over women was extremely well-received. A glossy magazine bought it from *Red Rag*, and he was invited to expand his views on *Woman's Hour*, and was duly fawned upon for his enlightened, pro-feminist opinions.

And then a publisher telephoned him and asked if he would like to do a book on Women's Liberation – from a supportive male stance. They thought they could sell it in America, too. Gerry was very interested in this prospect – after a foolish, impulsive episode when he had joined the Italian Communist Party (which he hardly counted as a Communist Party at all, and found a whole lot of fun) he had had a little difficulty with getting an American visa, but a sound publishing venture would surely nullify that.

Louisa and he went on seeing each other regularly, usually when he was in London once a week – and occasionally he stayed with her over a weekend. Their relationship was, certainly, curious. In their everyday friendship, as it were, they were cheerful and cordial, and although Louisa listened to Gerry when he talked politics, she assumed the dominant role in other respects: perhaps because when they were together, they lived in her home, and she regarded London as her territory. And she had that commanding, upper-class streak anyhow. But in their private, sexual relationships, she craved an almost pathological submission; she needed total physical domination and she liked to be struck.

Gerry wasn't always comfortable in his relationship with Louisa. Sometimes he asked himself why he continued with it. If he were to be honest with himself, he knew he was drifting a little, in his personal life, just going along in neutral gear. He liked Louisa well enough; she certainly had interesting complexities. She had a beautiful body and a well-educated mind. She was very decisive – he admired that. She now had some well-laid plans for other publishing ventures, and he had been impressed by the way she handled what was becoming a flourishing business. And, of course, it was a convenient relationship. He didn't see her all the time, but more or less when he chose. Moreover, he hadn't declared, in words or by implication, any commitment of fidelity or loyalty to her, so he was free to have other sexual experiences if he chose to.

With Brita – whom he still missed, her dear little concerned, serious face looking up at him when he came home – he had felt guilty at the temptation, sometimes yielded to, of sleeping with other women.

Because he lived with Brita, and because she had been so devoted to him, he knew he owed her, somehow, a kind of loyalty, even though they both talked airily about open-ended relationships. He felt bad about betraying Brita. He didn't feel bad about betraying Louisa. Louisa acted as though they owed each other nothing – that was the difference.

Funny, he thought as he lay on Louisa's sofa one Saturday morning, aimlessly reading *New Society*, the difference in these two feminist women. Brita had been a committed feminist; her weakness had been a compulsion to domestic order and the need to care for a man, to keep the kitchen floor spotless.

Louisa was a committed feminist; her weakness was that in the matter of sex, she desired a man to be a brute. Strange.

Louisa came in carrying a mug of coffee for him, and a glass of juice for herself.

'Thanks,' he grinned. 'Not having one?' he indicated the coffee.

She shook her head, and sat cross-legged on the floor, leaning on a hillock of Afghan cushions.

'I'm pregnant,' she explained simply. 'Coffee always makes me sick when I'm pregnant.'

'You're pregnant?' Gerry was utterly astonished. 'Is it mine?'

She looked at him impatiently 'Of course it's yours. I wouldn't be telling you about it if it weren't.'

'I see,' Gerry said thoughtfully. 'Well, well, well.' He was still in a state of surprise. It was not, curiously, unpleasant. It was curiously gratifying, in some strange way.

'I'll have the termination on Monday,' she said. 'It's early enough for an outpatient treatment. They do a very good job at the Paddington health authority. Under ten weeks, you just walk in, walk out.' She smiled. 'It's colloquially referred to as the lunchtime abortion. Though in fact their sessions are in the morning. You do rest up, of course. But you're out within a few hours.'

Gerry looked at his coffee. Louisa always made delicious coffee: grinding it from real beans, perking it in a real Italian coffee-maker. He tried to focus on the coffee, a psychological trick he had learned when feelings had to be controlled.

He focused on the coffee because he understood that in this particular episode he was being told that he was surplus to requirements. He was not even being called upon to play the male role of providing the cash. The state did that, within the National Health Service, particularly for those, like Louisa, who knew how to work the system.

'Do I come into the picture?' he asked quietly.

'No, Gerry, not at all,' Louisa said pleasantly, but with authority. 'Biologically, of course, your sperm fertilized my egg. You are, if you like to put it that way, the progenitor of the foetus. But what happens after that is my choice. We've always agreed on that. Heck, you've pointed that out many times when we've done campaigns. Your polemical position has never varied – has it?'

Gerry stood up, and fished in his trouser pocket for a cigarette paper.

'Sure,' he said. 'But it would be nice to be consulted.'

'Well, I've told you about it, haven't I?' Louisa said reasonably. 'Plenty of women don't bother to let the man know at all. That's the new trend. The woman just has the termination, and it's up to her whether she chooses to tell the man. It's her business, after all.'

He rolled his cigarette, concentrating on it. Gerry felt emotionally bewildered; he couldn't help it.

'I thought you were on the mini-pill,' he said. It was a reproach.

Louisa shrugged. 'The Pill – any Pill – doesn't really agree with me. I was planning to switch to an IUD. Sometimes they agree to inserting an IUD when they do the termination. I might do that.'

'I see,' he said. 'Just like that. You flush a foetus out of your body and you stick a bit of metal in. It's all a matter of mechanics, isn't it?'

'Look, Gerry,' Louisa said crossly, 'As far as I'm concerned, this is just an inconvenience which I'm about to remedy. I don't expect you, of all people, to go all reactionary and sentimental about a perfectly practical decision. So give over, will you?'

Gerry lit the thin little cigarette he had made with the Rizla paper.

'I'm not "going all reactionary". I just think I should have some choice too,' he said.

Louisa looked at him, astonished.

'If you wanted to choose to have a child, you should have told me so. You should have talked about it. You never expressed any such idea.'

'I don't know whether I want a child or not,' Gerry said

impatiently. 'But now that it has happened, I'd *like* to talk about it, yes. What difference does it make whether I told you before you got pregnant, or afterwards?'

'Because if you had told me before – that you wanted a child – I would have informed you, as I'm informing you now, Gerry, that there is no way I'm going to have your child. And if you'd known that, you would have had a choice – of wearing a French letter or having a vasectomy.'

Gerry stood up again and walked to the door. He was determined not to lose his temper, but he was very distressed inside. He looked back at her. 'Has this happened before?' he asked. 'Have you had other abortions?'

'Gerry!' she remonstrated. 'That's no business of yours whatsoever! It's *my body*.'

He left the room and went to the bedroom. There he picked up what belonged to him in Louisa's flat: three paperback books and an overnight shoulder bag. He put on his leather jacket and stubbed out the feeble little cigarette in a china dish.

He came back to the living-room door. 'I'm going home, Louisa,' he said. 'I want to think for a wee bit.'

'Fine,' she shrugged.

'By the way,' he said, as he was preparing to leave. 'Why don't you get the abortionist to beat you up before he sticks his other instruments into you? Then you can have the pleasure of an abortion and the pleasure of a kinky bit of masochism at the same time. Just up your street!'

She threw a book at him, ferociously. 'Get out!' she yelled. 'You horrible Irish oik! Get out of my house!'

He left.

Gerry went and sat by the canal for a while, before taking the tube to Liverpool Street for Colchester. He remembered the Grand Canal in Dublin, where he had done a post-graduate year. He used to walk by the banks of that Dublin canal with such a sweet young woman called Dervla. She was lovely: so young, soft, trusting, innocent, so untouched by all this modern knowingness and sophistication. He had parted with her on good terms – on the reasonable terms that he had to go abroad, and she had said goodbye to him so tearfully, so loyally. He had parted with most women he had known on good terms, really; at least, he had always managed some sort of gracious farewell. With Louisa, he reflected, throwing a pebble into the water, he had certainly come a cropper, well and truly. He was ashamed, thoroughly ashamed, at the cheapness and crudeness of his parting shot. That was the primitive unconscious rising up, all right. He was disgusted, too, that she had called him 'you Irish oik'. In temper, she had returned to form as well.

Maybe he should have beaten her up. Maybe she would have respected that, knowing her curious psychology. He had seen a quote she had cut out from a women's magazine, allegedly from something said by Zsa Zsa Gabor, on all non-feminist role-models: 'No woman has been truly loved until she has been truly beaten.' Maybe if he had beaten Louisa, she would have felt more loved, at that moment, and they would have understood each other better. But then again, he didn't want to beat her up. Beating women up was simply not at all to his taste. Why should he have to do something he didn't care for? That's a form of oppression too, after all.

He threw another stone into the water, watching the ripples. The trees were winter-bleak, bare, stripped. He felt odd about the pregnancy, too. He would have liked to be consulted – it wasn't an unreasonable request. Perhaps, deep down, he wanted to have the child. He tried to imagine what it would have been like. He thought, then, of all pregnancies announced with joy and celebration and happiness. That was the way his mother would have reacted. A child is always welcome, for some. Still, he had no right to think such thoughts. He had, after all, nailed his colours to the mast. He had always said it was a woman's choice, and it would be an act of humbug to claim any rights now.

Gerry didn't want to be a humbug. All the same, he couldn't quite help how he felt about it. Feelings weren't always easy to fit into the framework of rationality. They did break out, from time to time. And feminism was always saying, too, that it was *okay* to have feelings, that men should cry more. He certainly could have cried now.

Gerry rose from the canal-bank seat. Perhaps next weekend, he would go back to Belfast for a visit. Recharge his batteries. See some old friends. Ireland always brought back a sense of joy to his life, despite the troubles. A sense, paradoxically, of optimism. It occurred to him now, as he started walking towards the underground, that it was because there were always so many children about the place. Children were just natural, there.

There would be other times, other women, he reflected. His charm felt flat, squashed and dormant just now, but it would surely rise again to sweeten and cajole.

Eavesdroppers' Luck

It all began with the fuss over that novel *The Satanic Verses*. You may remember that it caused a great stir among some Muslims, and indeed the world at large. Few people could, apparently, understand the text of the book, but it became so notorious that people read it out of sheer curiosity. It was this common curiosity that animated me when I saw a copy of the novel lying in the back of my husband's Rover. I happened to be using his car because my own was being serviced.

Alan was at a conference at Harrogate for a couple of days, so I took the book into the house with me, intending to take a look at it later, in bed, with some Mozart on the compact disc and a comforting cup of camomile tea. Alan and I both have *very* busy lives – I am the director of an English-language school in London and he is a computer and software expert – so a quiet night alone at home with a couple of books is something soothing for me: not to have to go to a reception, not to have to talk to anyone . . .

As I began to peruse the pages of Mr Rushdie's celebrated novel, I began to see why some critics had called it 'impenetrable'. It was hard going; but we often have courses for Saudi Arabian students so I thought it would be useful for me to grasp the Islamic background, and I persisted. *Then* I saw that there was a piece of paper stuck into the middle of the book as a marker. I turned to the page thus marked, and saw that someone – not Alan – had scribbled in pencil, in the margin, 'the offending passage'. I remember noticing that it was page 381. I read the passage that had caused so much of the *furore*, an elliptical narrative about Mohammed appearing in a brothel, and felt that my curiosity had been sufficiently satisfied.

It was none of it very meaningful to a non-Muslim, and I was about to shut the book and take up the new Dick Francis, when I idly glanced at the piece of paper which had marked the page. It was a Barclaycard statement, and once again, it was sheer curiosity that prompted me to open it out and examine it.

This, of course, was a mistake, and I knew that instinctively. My grandmother, who was an American, always did say that folks who listen in to conversations not intended for their ears, or read documents not intended for their eyes, never learn well of themselves. 'Eavesdroppers' luck', she called it. This is apparently yet another of those old wives' superstitions which turn out to be based on the wisdom of experience. I should have known better than to look at that bill.

For, in addition to my grandma's *nostrums*, Alan and I had always agreed upon respecting each other's privacy. We regard ourselves as married equals, and we run three bank accounts: his, mine and ours. The common bank account, used for most 'together' costs, was open for inspection by either, but our personal accounts we kept to ourselves. Our marriage, which has until now been an entirely harmonious one – for over twelve years – has been based on the concept of balancing truthfulness with independence.

Most couples quarrel about either money or children. We determined we should never fight about money; and we agreed, right from the start, that we should remain childless by choice. In fact, I was sterilized five years ago, when I was thirty-one. The gynaecologist kept deferring the operation, arguing that I was too young to make such a final decision. But I was fed up with messing about with various forms of contraception, and I had been certain, for some years, that I did not want children. My mother was a hopelessly feckless woman who had been married three times, and had always ended up dumping her someone else – which had given me a strong aversion to motherhood.

I had been lucky to have known my grandmother, but she died when I was sixteen, leaving me feeling orphaned. Until I met Alan I had felt alone in the world, and I never wanted to spoil the security of our partnership by having babies.

Alan was absolutely happy – I always thought – to agree with my decision about this. He seemed as certain as I was that we would never want or need children. When we were discussing sterilization, it is true that the gyny mentioned that male vasectomy was clinically simpler than female sterilization. But I over-rode such objections, saying that it was my right to control my body as *I* wished, and this was the way that I chose to do it. In retrospect, however, I see that Alan didn't exactly push the question of vasectomy.

Money and families must have both hovered around my mind as I read my husband's credit card statement. There were just two items billed on it: one was for £38.50 for lunch in Soho, which was not unusual. It was the second item which held my attention. This was a billing from the Margaret Sanger Family Planning Clinic for £380.

I knew of the Margaret Sanger clinic. My colleagues had mentioned recommending it to some of our overseas students who enquired about birth control facilities in London. But what on earth was Alan doing at a birth control clinic? I looked at the date of the bill: it was just four weeks previously. Thoughtfully, I placed the statement back inside *The Satanic Verses*, just as I had found it, folded in three, neatly tucked into page 381. I then poured myself a substantial Glenfiddich and planned what I would do about this the following morning.

I called my secretary early and said I had an unexpected working breakfast with a Japanese client. Then I picked up my own car from the garage, looked up the address of the Margaret Sanger Clinic, and drove to Euston.

I had rehearsed carefully what I was going to say, but I felt

149

uncharacteristically nervous as I powdered my face before leaving the car on a meter.

The receptionist had clearly been hired for her pleasantness, and when I said I wanted to make some enquiries, she directed me to a young woman she called Kim. Kim was to be found in a room marked 'private counselling' – a rather beautiful, demure girl with violet eyes. She, too, had been trained to be friendly to those who approached her with some uncertainty, and said immediately that I had come along at a very good time – first thing on a Friday morning. Well, I told her, I didn't really require very much. It was just, I explained, that I was a teacher and at a recent European meeting of educationalists, some Spanish women had approached me about family planning services in London – and I wanted to help them. Kim smiled – she smiled a great deal – and said how happy the Margaret Sanger would be to provide all the information and assistance that might be necessary.

She explained what was on offer: contraception; sterilization – male and female; artificial insemination by donor; and termination of pregnancy. She began to take up some leaflets with prices and procedures explained in that neutral language which hides the drama that exists behind these decisions. Kim kept smiling, all the while. She was selling a product, after all. 'We're very competitive,' she said. 'Our prices have altered very little over the past four years, and we have very high health standards. A recent survey shows that we have a lower post-operative infection rate than the National Health Service.'

'Post-operative?' I asked.

'For . . . termination of pregnancy,' Kim looked coy as a geisha.

'Ah,' I said. It was as though something had slotted into place, as when you watch a billiard-ball find its targeted hole.

I looked at the price list. It just said 'Termination of pregnancy – from £140.'

'Can you give me more details about prices?' I asked Kim.

'Sure thing,' said Kim. 'In the first trimester of pregnancy, the price is £140, plus £40 for the doctor's consultation. That's

150

kids on someone else – which had given me a strong aversion to an outpatient service. After twelve weeks, the cost goes up because the operation is more complicated, and there has to be an overnight stay. That's £275.'

'Is that the top price?' I asked, adding quickly – 'Spanish ladies can't always get to London in a hurry.'

'We have another rate for very late cases,' Kim added. 'That is, for a pregnancy between 20 and 23 weeks. It is not really an advisable operation, but there are special needs sometimes.'

'How much,' I asked, in a rather steely way, 'is this five-month abortion?'

'£380 in all,' said Kim, ever smiling. 'By the way, we take credit cards,' she added helpfully.

I knew they took credit cards, of course. Rage, resentment, bile and jealousy all mingled together in me like a horrible whirlpool.

'Nobody likes to do this operation,' said Kim. 'But there can be very compelling reasons.'

'What sort of reasons?' I asked. Then I said, qualifying my question, 'As a teacher, I hope I'd be able to handle this problem if it ever cropped up with one of our pupils.'

'It may well occur,' smiled Kim. 'Young girls, schoolgirls, who have hidden their pregnancies are often candidates for these late terminations of pregnancy. Then there are women from overseas – we have many clients from Spain. The ones I find most tragic of all, personally, are those women who've wanted a pregnancy until their man suddenly turns against them and persuades them to terminate. You'd be surprised at the number of men who suddenly can't face fatherhood; or the number who are married, and suddenly decide, at the last possible moment, that they are not going to leave their wife.'

'Tragic,' I agreed, feeling my nostrils flaring, as they do when I am exerting emotional control.

'Then,' said Kim, 'there are the ones who are just testing their fertility. Some men only allow a pregnancy to happen – well, some women also – in order to prove to themselves that they are capable of having a child.

'They are initially pleased when the pregnancy occurs. It is only when they begin to see the bump that the reality of the situation sinks in. Then they decide they can't face it.'

'Do you ever counsel them to think again?' I asked, again from curiosity.

Kim looked mildly shocked. 'Oh, we never interfere with clients' decisions. It's their choice, after all. That's what they're paying for.'

I stood up. 'Thank you, you've been very helpful,' I said, taking the leaflets.

'It's nice to talk to another person in the caring professions,' smiled Kim. 'I hope we can offer our services to any of your Spanish friends who might need us.'

She put a slight emphasis on 'your Spanish friends'. As I left the clinic, I wondered if she had spotted me for a fake, like those pathetic individuals who ask for a pornographic book 'for a friend'. That was precisely how I felt, for some reason.

However, I didn't care all that much what Kim thought of me. As I walked back to my car, my preoccupations were elsewhere. My husband, from whom I had no secrets, had paid for an abortion for some woman, four weeks ago. Not only an abortion, but a damnably late abortion too. If he had paid for it, it almost certainly meant he was responsible for the pregnancy. And if so, for how long had he been conducting an affair? If the pregnancy was over twenty weeks, that was a lot of time, in my book. And why had the woman in question decided to have an abortion so late?

Was it something to do with what Kim had said about men testing out their fertility, and then panicking when the pregnancy became visible? As I had always taken the initiative in birth control, Alan had never had the opportunity to put his procreative powers to the test. Yet he had never seemed to mind about it; or, should I say, he had never seemed *to me* to mind about it?

It is more than two weeks now since I found that Barclaycard statement of Alan's, and I still haven't been able to bring myself to ask him about it. Indeed, I behaved in the classically guilty eavesdropper's way – I put *The Satanic Verses* back in Alan's car, exactly where I had found it, as though it had never been disturbed. Then, when the *furore* about that novel rumbled on, Alan mentioned that there was a copy of it in the Rover, which someone at work had lent him. I said I must look at it, casually, and so he gave it to me, the next time he was bringing some papers into the house from the car. I took it up, as though for the first time, and began to look through it again. But page 381 now had nothing marking it. The statement had gone.

I am a very controlled person – that's how I got to be successful in my job – and I think have been able to dissimulate my anger, even hatred, during these couple of weeks. As is usual, we have both been very busy – both in London and on the various trips we both of us make outside of it – and there has been no special opportunity to confront him about the Margaret Sanger matter anyway. He must notice that I am less responsive to him – but then, did I notice, over the past six months or so, that he was less responsive to me? Was I too preoccupied to pay attention, too independent?

Another of my grandmother's sayings was 'don't get mad – get even' and I have formulated a plan for getting even, too. I have been back to talk to another counsellor at Margaret Sanger – Kim was on holiday – about the possibility of reversing a sterilization operation. The counsellor thinks it is tricky, but possible, and I am considering having it done while allegedly on a business trip to Mexico. Then perhaps *I* will surprise Alan with a pregnancy.

Only then, when I am in a position to get even, a position of equals, of tit for tat, will I be able to bring up that matter of the bill I should never have examined.

Give it Time

Occasionally I catch a glimpse of Vanessa Phillips in the King's Road area of Chelsea, that haunt of 1960s activity which remains, to me, so remarkably unchanged twenty years on. For a while, our children – Vanessa's son and my son and daughter – even attended the same school, although I never made myself known to Vanessa. I never went over to her and said, 'Hi, Vanessa, I'm Rachel. Remember me? Rachel McGowan, as was.' I knew that she was both short-sighted and vague; she was not the sort of person to spot me across the school playground, thinking 'I know that face.' Even if she had seen me up close, she might not recognize me or quite recall who I was. I have changed a lot in the twenty years since our lives intermingled. Moreover, whenever I have caught sight of Vanessa, she has been with her son, apparently wholly absorbed by him. As though he now represented her whole world.

Vanessa's appearance has faded a little, of course, and she seems more nervous, less self-confident than she had been when I first knew her. But then, she has lived through those turbulent years of a woman's life that encompass the span from the twenties to the forties. And her marriage seems to have failed, which I always think saps a person's confidence, at least for a while.

Is it gratifying to us, more ordinary-looking mortals, to reflect that time and fortune wound the beautiful, the socially well-placed and the well-to-do just as much as it batters about the rest of us, poor bloody infantry? Perhaps it appeals to our childish sense of justice, this knowledge that we are all equal before the ravages of time; perhaps it abates the raging envy we might otherwise feel for those who seem to be born in such favourable circumstances.

Vanessa and I had originally met as two young women both involved with two brothers, Jake and Andy Phillips. We might, at one stage, have become sisters-in-law – or so I hoped, although any such hopes turned out to be pure fancy.

It also happened that we were from the same part of Ireland, which caused some people to imagine that we might be acquainted, or have affinities in some respect. Old Mrs Phillips – Jake and Andy's mother – never made that error, however. She perceived immediately the difference in our background. She appreciated Vanessa's pedigree, and ignored mine. Vanessa was, after all, the daughter of Sir Henry Knowle, and had a family home in County Down which was one of the minor joys of Ulster architecture: a Georgian manor house which her Scottish ancestors had built with the spoils of having 'pacified' (pacified!) Ireland. Whereas I came from a small town in County Armagh, the only child of a widowed schoolteacher.

Vanessa and I were almost neighbours, back home in Northern Ireland, yes, and we were both Protestants too. I dread to think how much more scorn old Mrs Phillips might have poured on me if I had been a Papist, to boot! Yet being Protestant in Ireland doesn't by any means imply being of a similar rank. Being county folk, Vanessa's parents were Church of Ireland, while my parents had been strict and simple Baptists, modest in social standing, completely unpretentious. Border Baptists in Ireland were also traditionally more 'Irish'. My father knew the Irish language, and loved Irish traditional music. Whereas Vanessa's people were, in most ways, indistinguishable from their cousins in Gloucestershire.

Mrs Phillips was thrilled to pieces, of course, that her loutish younger son, Andy, had effected such a catch. The daughter of an Anglo-Irish grandee; such good connections! Andy himself was what we would call today a Hooray Henry. He was loud, boisterous, an unbearable braggart and a painfully embarrassing practical joker. I was quite puzzled as to what it was that attracted Vanessa to Andy. Now, with the experience of years, I understand. It was this: Andy cheered her up. He made her laugh. And it is a well-established fact that any man who can make a woman laugh has her in the palm of his hand.

Andy's cheerful loutishness amused Vanessa, particularly as it was in such contrast to her own family life, which was gloomy and lugubrious. I once went to a party at Castlewellan, Vanessa's family home. I thought her people were awful – her father glowering and forbidding, her mother introverted and neurotic, and her brother a prize bigot in a land where the competition for bigotry can be extremely stiff. I am ashamed to say that I was not wholly distressed when the IRA took a pot shot at him, after the Troubles of the 1970s began, which left him partly paralysed. This is a dreadful admission to make, but we all have unkindly thoughts sometimes, and I am afraid that I have a streak of real malice.

In any case, Vanessa had fallen for Andy Phillips, hook, line and sinker. They had met, first, at Glasgow University, and had then come down to London at the same time. Vanessa had dabbled in the antiques and auctioneering business, while Andy became – wouldn't you know! – an estate agent. He was shrewd enough to see, even in the 1960s, that the property boom was going to be good for those in real estate.

The curious thing was that Andy's mother – and his elder brother, Jake – rather disapproved of this line of business he had chosen, despite his initial success in it. People are, I have learned, full of paradoxes and strange, contradictory foibles. The Phillips family were of a socialist tradition: the father – though dead by the time I became involved with Jake – had been a Labour Member of Parliament for a brief period after 1945. They disapproved, somewhat priggishly, of what they called 'property speculators', and in that bracket they included estate agents. The Welsh are touchy about property, in a daft egalitarian sort of way. It is strange, though, is it not, that they didn't disapprove of Sir Henry Knowle, who was, after all a landlord? Oh no! Something happens to people when they become involved with the nobility, however minor. They are wooed and seduced by it, somehow. And then there is a funny sort of snobbery which disdains brash new money, but accepts old money that may well have been gained by piracy and plunder – which makes the freelance gazumper pretty petty stuff.

And so Mrs Phillips would gush, and bill, and coo, over Vanessa; Vanessa the beautiful – and yes, Vanessa was rather a beauty, with more than a passing resemblance to a pop singer of the time, Marianne Faithfull. Vanessa the kind – all the works she did for charity, don't you know! Vanessa the accomplished – why, she played the harp, and the piano, and made all her own clothes just for the pleasure of it. 'And the reception will, of course, be at Castlewellan House,' Mrs Phillips went over and over the plans in advance. 'And they're going to have the Marquess of Dungannon as the best man!' Her voice would become squeaky with excitement. 'It's all wonderful, isn't it?'

I was, I remember, ready to weep with envy at the time. My relationship with Andy's brother, Jake, seemed so unsatisfactory in comparison to this fairytale romance. I was stupidly, crazily, and destructively smitten by Jake who – as in all cases of one-sided ardour – returned my devotion with a certain patronising air. For him, I was *a* girlfriend. He didn't mind going to bed with me, and spending evenings with me when it suited him. And he was quite good about introducing me to his family – unlike some Englishmen, he didn't regard his family as a private vice which you do not mix with your social connections. But I don't think, now, that I was anything very special to Jake. Whereas for at least two years of my life, he was everything to me. I look back now and remember how my heart would do a flip when I glimpsed him coming into a restaurant or a cinema to meet me. What was it about him? He was ordinary-looking; curly brown hair, beard, glasses, rather good blue eyes. Yet I can't count the times when – for years and years afterwards – I would turn my head to examine the faces of men with beards and glasses and curly brown hair.

He was very different from his brother, in temperament; rather quiet and reserved, controlled, on the surface. I like quiet men, on the supposition (not always verified) that quiet people have hidden depths. Jake had hidden depths, all right. He could be very cruel. He had this idea that jealousy was something we had now done away with.

Primitive peoples like the Sicilians were jealous, and characters in nineteenth-century novels were jealous; and there was the matter of Othello. But this was the 1960s, and we were the liberated generation who lived in London, the world's most civilized city. We could do away with jealousy. I thought this a frightfully new, radical idea at the time: I have since come across the same ideas in stories about decadent life in the 1930s: indeed in the eighteenth century. People are forever discovering something modern and new, when it has all been thought of before.

But of course, being twenty-two, and being so completely under Jake's influence, I swallowed all this, and tried my best to live up to his cool view that jealousy had been done away with. I found it very hard not to be jealous, especially when Jake gave me such reason for so much pain. As part of his personal and social experiment on the non-existence of jealousy, he would talk quite openly about his other relationships. It drove me nearly crazy. He would leave evidence around his flat of other girls having been there – notes, tights, powder compacts. He would stock, say, Lapsang tea in his kitchen, saying casually: 'Oh, Ursula likes Lapsang tea. I keep it for whenever she comes over.' Ursula was a voluptuous, extrovert, laughing woman who worked in television. There was another woman called Carla, with whom he had had an on-off affair for some years. I remember finding a letter – opened, left lying around – from Carla, a passionate letter to Jake in which she wrote of how close she felt to him when he was inside her, how utterly amoeba-like she felt . . . God: I remember the rage, the overpowering wave of jealousy, then the cold feeling of rejection and despair that crept all over me. I understand why people murder: I really do. If I could have murdered Carla at that moment, I would have done.

At twenty-two, I just didn't have the experience to cope with these emotions, to live up to Jake's sophisticated ban on jealousy, while I felt this passionate attachment, this obsession for him. And then I felt this extra envy for the sort of relationship that his brother Andy enjoyed with his fiancée, Vanessa. Theirs was a larky, merry courtship, and they seemed untroubled and united.

Taking her cue from her sons' general attitudes, Mrs Phillips treated me quite differently from the way she fawned upon Vanessa. She could, obviously, see that her eldest son was not about to settle down permanently with this inconsequential little travel clerk – I worked in a humble capacity in a small travel agency, at the time – and she all too obviously regarded me as just another casual girlfriend. She never once asked after my family, or expressed the slightest concern when my lone mother had a slight stroke and I had to rush to get a plane to Belfast. Whereas with Vanessa – well, endless solicitous enquiries were made about the health and prosperity of her family.

I was actually quite surprised to be invited to the engagement party for Vanessa and Andy. Surprised, because by that time I felt quite outside the Phillips family circle; and I didn't feel close to Vanessa, either. She had always been courteous towards me, even cordial, but it went no further than that. Whether it was the social gap between our backgrounds, or the psychological gap between our status in regard to our men – she an established fiancée, I a casual girlfriend – I do not know. Andy's attitude to me could be maddening, though at base there was no harm in it. But he was forever cracking idiotic Irish jokes and doing 'funny' Irish voices; this can be droll once or twice, but there is a certain stupid kind of English person who continues to think it is funny the hundredth time. Andy was like that. Moreover, by the time the engagement party was imminent, my relationship with Jake had become distinctly rocky. The pattern consisted of urgent sessions in bed, followed by rows, followed by me apologizing, followed by urgent sessions in bed.

I didn't know a lot when I was twenty-two, but I knew enough to realize that our relationship was deteriorating, and that gradually I was losing Jake – or whatever little part of him I had once had. I knew it but I did not want to face it. I remember the moment of truth quite distinctly. I was sitting on the top deck of a number nine bus, which was moving through Kensington. I had just been to Biba's boutique in Ken Church Street. There had been a gramophone record playing – in those days it was records, not taped music – and it had expressed what I knew, deep down.

It was Dusty Springfield – or was it Cilla Black? – singing 'You've Lost that Loving Feeling'. It repeated and repeated in my head, and as the bus passed the park and I saw the crocuses just beginning to flower, I thought – that's it. He has lost that loving feeling. Woe, woe, woe . . .

At the engagement party for Vanessa and Andy, I became miserably drunk, which is not like me: alcohol does not agree with me physically, and I feel ashamed, somehow, of betraying my family's strict teetotal tradition. I do well recall watching the burgeoning trees from the Hyde Park Hotel, and feeling so extremely sorry for myself. Loss and rejection in youth is inconsolable, for there is a total draining-away of self-esteem thereby. In later life, people can take set-backs and disappointments a little more philosophically, but a love-affair that goes wrong at a tender age is misery.

I hated the people at that party too, with their loud whinnying laughs and brash greeting-calls. The mixture of gentry, estate agents and Oxbridge socialists was most infelicitous, I thought. And I hardly knew anyone. Jake hated me being drunk too, and scarcely spoke to me. I stood around forlornly, watching Mrs Phillips flannelling and fawning over the Marquess of Dungannon, a pale, bespectacled, blond young

161

man. Tarquin Dungannon was very grand indeed – connected by marriage to a whisky fortune, and by distinct kinship, to the Royal Family through the Earls of Strathmore, the Queen Mother's family. He was also a fashionable figure in the world of the arts, an innovator, an art critic, and owned a London gallery which sold contemporary work. He had brought many of the contemporary New York artists to London, including Lichtenstein and Warhol.

I softened slightly when I saw Vanessa and Andy dancing together. They did seem so serenely happy, blissfully in love, an effervescent young couple with every good prospect before them. Then the English Hooray Henrys and the Irish swells started shrieking their heads off once again and I turned back to the dreaming trees of Hyde Park, and another fill of vodka and tonic.

The wedding took place that summer. I was not invited, as Jake and I had well and truly broken up by then. Yet I had good reason to remember the date. As Vanessa and Andy were walking down the aisle of the tiny, picturesque Church of Ireland in her parish in County Down, I was checking into a clinic in Devonshire Place, London, to have an abortion. It was ludicrous, wasn't it? Yet it was precisely the sort of thing that women do when they are desperate.

As Jake began to slip from me, as I heard that song about losing that loving feeling play repeatedly in my inner ear, consciously or unconsciously, I made my last gamble. Consciously or unconsciously, as we spent a final weekend together in the Welsh mountains – Jake actually had the coolness to announce that it was a 'goodbye treat' for me – I left my contraceptive pills lying in the bathroom of my Hammersmith flat. Consciously or unconsciously, I took the risk of getting pregnant, as a way to hold – or perhaps just to test – Jake. Naturally, it didn't work. If a relationship is on the way down, pregnancy hardly ever holds it together. I know that now. But when you're twenty-two, you obey impulses, and some of these are partly biological. I loved Jake. I wanted to get pregnant. I took the risk. And extraordinarily, I did get pregnant.

He was brutal in his reaction. He was not flattered that I had made this gesture. He was just extremely irritated. He made a slicing sound with his mouth and a cutting mime with his hand. 'Get it out,' he said succinctly. 'It's just like going to the dentist: it is just another extraction.' The fee for the abortion arrived from him, in a plain brown envelope. Two hundred and fifty guineas, to be precise. And three words of farewell that I could hardly bear to contemplate, then, or for a long time after. Did I cry!

Following the perversities of fate, I stopped off at the Portland Street Post Office on the way to the clinic, to send a telegraph of good wishes to Andy and Vanessa for their wedding reception. I did wish them well, truly, and hoped that Andy's schoolboy spirits would always cheer Vanessa, and that her misty, ethereal beauty would continue to shimmer for him. The telegram was a goodbye for me, in many respects. A goodbye to Jake. A goodbye to his baby. A goodbye to a certain era of my life. As the sun glinted on the morning streets of London, I thought about the time and the emotion I had spent on Jake: the anguish of waiting for him to telephone me, of swearing I wouldn't abase myself by phoning him again, and then, of finding the separation so searing, of picking up that telephone and all but begging to see him. Oh God, I swore: help me to change myself, to stop being such a victim, so helpless in the grip of love and passion. Help me to get over this mistake, and start again, to change . . .

People do not, of course change overnight, and sometimes they do not change at all – despite the promises of the self-improvement books. But sometimes, they do gradually develop, especially after an experience which touches them at a deep level. I suffered over that abortion: it wasn't just the loss of the baby, but the rejection, the sense of failure, the lowering of self-esteem. The clinic was swanky and yet the nurses – I never saw the consultant again into whose well-manicured hands I had pressed the 250 guineas, on initial consultation – the nurses gave the impression of not caring a lot about the job they were doing. There was something extremely depressing about every aspect of that well-appointed establishment.

I emerged the following morning with my overnight bag, feeling very alone and very determined somehow to learn from this shattering experience, and be constructive about the rest of my life. I determined to concentrate on my work for a while, to put my emotional life on one side. I might only be a humble travel clerk, I reckoned, but I did like the business, and it had enormous possibilities. A friend of mine used to go with her family to a Greek island – at that time a totally unspoiled and hugely exotic part of the Aegean. I decided to ask her if I could spend a week there.

And when I saw its beauty – and its tourist possibilities – I decided to ask her to help me start a travel agency that would specialize in Greek and Yugoslav tours. Her family had the money to invest, and together we persuaded the Midland Bank to lend us more. A fascinating career then opened up for me: in fact, I've never looked back.

It was at a summer party, in an Islington garden many summers later, that I took up the thread of Vanessa and Andy's life.

'You're Rachel McGowan, aren't you?' said a pleasant, slightly plump woman in her forties, seated next to me on a terrace chair. Standing at parties is boring. I always sit down: people come and join you, that way. 'We met twenty years ago,' she explained. 'My husband Charlie was at Cambridge with Jake Phillips – do you remember? You were with Jake at the time. We had dinner together in Jake's flat.'

I looked at this comely matron, astonished – not for the first time – that so many of my contemporaries were beginning to look older, which meant that I must be showing my age too. Yes, I had seen her before somewhere, though I could not have said exactly where or when. She went on to prompt me with her name and background. She was called Paulene Maitland. Her husband Charlie had been, more or less, Jake's best friend. They used to get together, often with other Cambridge contemporaries, and talk enthusiastically about planning and design, either over a *chilli con carne* which I (or some other woman) would produce, or else at a restaurant in the King's Road called, I think, 351. Seeing Paulene now, so much came back to me that I had wiped clean from the video of memory.

I had not kept in touch with Jake, although I had heard in a circuitous way that he had married. And it afforded me some mean-spirited satisfaction to have learned, too, that the marriage was childless. He had, after all, rejected my child-that-would-have been. It was his own fault, in a way, that he now had no children. I hoped that he took the point: you don't always get second chances.

'Do you still see Jake?' Paulene asked me.

No, I explained. I had spent so much of my time travelling in the intervening years that I had lost touch with many old friends. It was only since my children began school that I had properly settled in London.

'What about you?' I said to Paulene. 'Are you and your husband still friendly with him?'

'Oh yes,' nodded Paulene. 'Charlie even works with him occasionally. You'll recall – Charlie is an architect and Jake is now in town planning. So their careers are quite congruent.'

Jake would go into town planning, I thought. He liked organizing other people's lives, in that cool, reserved way. Imposing horrible municipal buildings on people is a wonderful way of showing your power, too.

'That's nice,' I said congenially. 'I hope he's happy.' Did I? Really?

'He seems content, in a way,' Paulene went on. 'Of course, he has had his problems. I suppose we all have had. His wife, Stephanie, was disappointed not to have produced babies and I think that caused some unhappiness for both of them. But they have weathered it, and I think, accepted it. Jake's main worry has been his brother.'

'Oh – Andy?'

'Yes, Andy. Andy rather went to the bad. He's been drinking like a fish for years. Lost his job, ran up a lot of debts. His wife left him after repeated broken promises on his part: you know how it is with alcoholics. They promise to reform, but they seldom do, unless they go and get themselves some professional help. Then I gather that Andy's wife, Vanessa, has family worries of her own – crushing death duties, and her mother, I understand, committed suicide. Jake feels very responsible for Andy, and of course for old Mrs Phillips, it has all been wretched. She had such high hopes of the marriage. And then Vanessa is being difficult about their child – won't agree to access and so on.'

'What a chapter of misfortune!' I said. It did strike me as a run of very bad luck indeed, though Lady Knowle's suicide was not unexpected, since she had tried it several times before.

'Yes, it's awful,' Paulene said compassionately. 'Some people seem to have *great* misfortunes. Jake thinks that Andy's divorce is especially hard on his mother, since she never now gets to see her only grandchild. It's too bad, really. Though I daresay Vanessa has her reasons.'

Yes, I thought, but if one of her sons had married me – well, I wouldn't have been like that. *I'd* have made sure Mrs Phillips saw her grandchild. We always think that we would behave better than others do, don't we?'

'Ever since we met at Jake's, I thought it would be nice to meet you again,' Paulene was saying. 'In fact, to be honest, I was rather disappointed that you and Jake didn't stay together.'

I liked this woman, I decided. She was on my side.

As we rode home to Chelsea later that evening, my husband asked what made me so silent.

'Just thinking about old times,' I said inconsequentially. 'Met a woman I used to know slightly, and we caught up on the doings of mutual friends.'

I was sorry, genuinely sorry, to learn that Andy and Vanessa had split up, because the end of a marriage brings a sort of universal disillusionment, and Andy's drink problems must have caused a lot of suffering. It is sad to think that two people can be so in love, so happy, when they first marry; and that they can come to dislike each other so much within a few years. I wondered, of course, whether I would have done any better, if I had married Jake. I had loved him – desperately, obsessively. But had I really *liked* him? I was more inclined, now, to dwell on his negative characteristics. I remembered how mean he was, for instance. How he had tried to get me to get him free, or reduced-rate, air tickets when he was planning to take another girlfriend – Ursula, I think – for a weekend in Majorca, although my job was such a modest little one in the travel agency business at the time. Even on our last weekend together in Wales, I had paid my half of the hotel bill. Granted, he had funded the abortion, but that was because he wanted to make sure I would go through with it.

I could feel a sort of abstract sympathy for old Mrs Phillips, though her haughty treatment of me still rankled a little.

Curious, though, how things work on a sort of synchronicity in life. You lose touch with a circle of people for years, and then news of them comes all at once.

Three days after my chat with Paulene Maitland, I opened the *Daily Mail* and read that the Marquess of Dungannon had died of AIDS. I remembered how Mrs Phillips had gushed over him. Although he was liked and respected in the arts world, he had been a promiscuous homosexual. It must have been another blow, in a way. The revelation of his lifestyle would not have gone down well with Mrs Phillips, I imagined.

The next time I glimpse Vanessa, I have resolved, I will stop and talk to her. I would like to befriend her again, for she has had so much bad luck. I will tell Dmitri to pull up the Mercedes, and I will get out and talk to her. If I get to know her well again, she might appreciate a holiday in one of our Greek villas. I would be generous enough, I think, either to offer it to her free, or at a *greatly* reduced rate.

Election Night: or The Road to Margaret Thatcher

15 October 1964

Picture, if you will, a roomy, untidy mansion flat in Earl's Court. Posters of the Beatles and The Who adorn the walls, as does a picture of Marlon Brando on a motorbike. In the bathroom, there is a mini-skirt hanging up to dry, and there are two packets of contraceptive pills propped up on the open-shelf medicine cabinet.

It is polling day. The four girls living here will go out and vote today.

'At least I hope we'll all go out to vote today,' says Jane, firmly, at breakfast. 'Remember Emily Davidson, the Suffragette, who threw herself under a racehorse so that we could have the vote.' Jane was head girl at Leeds Grammar School and has not forgotten her training in leadership and responsibility. Jane is going to be a teacher so she will certainly vote Labour. Jane is against grammar schools because they are so unfair. She admires Anthony Crosland, who swore: 'I'll abolish the grammar schools, if it's the last fucking thing I do!' (It was, more or less.)

Jane's exhortation is not wasted on Eileen, her dark-haired, pretty Irish flatmate. Eileen will certainly use her vote. Eileen has been to university in Belfast and she is now at drama school in London.

Eileen has also been on a demonstration in Derry, Northern

Ireland, where a kindly mixture of academics and intellectuals have held a peaceful march for fairer allocation of university opportunities between Catholics and Protestants. Such a good sign, these peaceful marches, thinks Eileen. Surely Harold Wilson, the Leader of the Labour Party, will sweep away the corrupt old practices in Northern Ireland and lead the way to a more democratic society there. Surely.

Sensible Jane and pretty Eileen get to the polls early. Jocasta, the third flat-mate is desperately busy and will try to squeeze voting in at some stage of her hectic day. Jocasta is a hospital doctor – a houseman, that is, often working a hundred hours a week. For this she earns £14 10s.3d. (Her sister, a secretary, earns £15 0s.0d.) Jocasta complains about being broke, she complains about being tired, but she is a dedicated doctor. She would like to see medicine become more democratic, however, to see a decline in the sort of male medicine where grand consultants speak down to the patients. She also finds time to campaign for the legalization of abortion – and to speak out against those Harley Street specialists who will not support legal abortion openly, yet continue to do it privately at 300 guineas a time.

Busy Jocasta will certainly vote Labour.

Flora, the last of the quartet, does not get to the polling station until the end of the day. She is in two minds about voting *at all*. Flora is an active Trotskyist. She is dismissive of bourgeois democracy and all its shams. She sometimes considers Labour worse than Conservative, for making concessions to the capitalist system while claiming to be socialist.

Flora was brought up in India by parents who served in the Raj. Through the benefices of her maternal grandmother, a fierce Scots dowager called Lady Gordon, Flora enjoys a considerable private income. The flat in which the four girls live belongs to Flora's family, and each of the girls pays Flora £7 a month in rent. Being a *rentier* makes Flora uncomfortable, but it is sensible Jane who insists. 'After all,' remonstrates Jane, 'charity perpetuates capitalism.' Being so well-informed, Jane is aware of Marxist theory. Flora defers to Jane, who has emerged as the natural leader, or at least the organizer, of the household.

Today, Flora lies in bed smoking a joint of cannabis, vacillating between voting and not voting. She is more excited by Mary Rand winning the Silver Medal at the Tokyo Olympics than by any bourgeois politics. Mary Rand has struck a blow for women.

In the end, a telephone conversation with her friend Roz convinces Flora that she should rouse herself and vote. Roz argues that Tories exploit women more, that it was typical Tory tactics to smear Christine Keeler, an honest working-class girl, to hide upper-class male decadence. Flora gets to the polls just before they close, after drinking a few rounds with Roz and another friend, Jo, at The Coach and Horses.

When Flora gets home around 10 p.m., she finds the other three sitting around the TV set watching the results, sharing a bottle of wine which cost 10s. 6d. from the local off-licence. On screen, Llew Gardner discusses the day's voting, while Robert McKenzie predicts the results with his swingometer. Soon after the polls close, it is announced that the Russian leader, Nikita Khrushchev, has 'resigned'; and that it looks like a Labour victory.

Eileen opens a fresh packet of cigarettes in excitement: 4s. 2d. for twenty. The girls' faces are lighted by the TV screen – young, alert, hopeful.

31 March 1966

By the time Election Night arrived again, sensible Jane had settled into such a nice, steady relationship with such a nice, steady young man, Roy. He was a good-humoured Manchester bloke who had been trained as a printer. He had come to London looking for work, but found it impossible to break into the closed shop of the London print unions. Still, he got the odd freelance job around the Home Counties. He was thinking of setting up in his own business.

On the March day that Harold Wilson once again went to

the country, Jane and Roy put down the payment for a flat in Notting Hill Gate. For someone as level-headed as Jane, her friends find the decision extraordinary. £5,000 for a London flat! Seems very extravagant.

Jocasta has completed her houseman's stint; she is still working at the London teaching hospital, though her hours now are a bit more civilised. She means to be a gynaecologist. Jocasta is a tall, wiry, blonde with a weakness for small, clever, Jewish men.

Despite her punishing schedule – she is involved in lots of activities outside work – she has managed to fit in quite a few of these characters. And it was to be at an election party that she was destined to meet the definitive model.

The election party is in Hampstead – very smart, very 60s. Jocasta meets the Jay twins, Germaine Greer, Mark Boxer and Richard Neville. It is all very scintillating. But it is Max Frenchman who really excites Jocasta. He is a small, clever, Jewish venerealogist, with a wry, corny line of patter ('They call me Max the Pox Doc, ha-ha!') and a lot of sweet-natured appeal. Jocasta is thoroughly enchanted. Still, she remembers to telephone Flora at the flat – FLAxman 2328 – and trills 'Happy election night, sister!' down the line.

'Come and join us, you dear old Trot!' she adds encouragingly.

But Flora won't go out tonight. She thinks it appalling that after two years of a Labour government, men and women still aren't equal. The average wage for women is still only £9 11s. 7d. a week, while that for men is £19 3s. 8d. She decides to abstain from voting. Jo, her friend, prefers to toast Cassius Clay's victory at Maple Leaf Gardens Stadium in Toronto rather than Wilson's predicted second win. Roz also turns up at Flora's, carrying the latest controversial best-seller: Bryan Magee's searing study of homosexuality in Britain in 1966, *One in Twenty*.

Eileen is no longer living at the Earl's Court flat. She is now touring in rep. She calls Flora in the evening, just before the show – a David Mercer play at Guildford – just to say hello.

172

Eileen is rather more emotionally concerned with her complicate private life than with politics. She is having an unhappy love affair with an actor who is married, with three children. Will he ever leave his wife? If only the divorce laws were easier!

Jane and Roy celebrate their mortgage by going to the pictures, to see *The Battle of the Bulge* at the Casino, and snogging most of the way through. They have slept together – Jane is on the Pill – but they have not yet lived together. It is not the usual thing to do, in 1966. But they will marry in the new financial year.

They have a wonderful meal at a South Kensington trattoria, which comes to £2 17s.6d., including wine.

18 June 1970

'In the last four years,' Jane writes in her diary, 'so much has happened!' And so it has. She has been teaching in a tough school in Dagenham, where it astonishes Jane to learn that most children haven't the slightest interest in learning, couldn't care less about the school system and only want to earn money as quickly as possible.

Jane and Roy have had a baby. They have sub-let their Notting Hill Gate flat to Jane's sister, and moved to Essex. Roy has started up his own business, publishing magazines.

Jocasta's relationship with Max Frenchman has continued, if stormily. They are a sparky pair anyway, but their workload introduces special stresses. As a venerealogist, Max is accustomed to an easy life. There is not a lot of work involved, and most people with an attack of VD are quickly cured. It suits his nature. He likes making people better. 'You give the sods a few drugs, tell them to behave themselves for a few weeks, and they go away happy. What more could a doctor want?'

Jocasta, on the other hand, has continued to work hard, as a gynaecologist. She was delighted when abortion became legal in 1968, but it did add to her workload. Safer abortion meant more abortion. And a more personal approach to childbirth was more labour-intensive too, as Max punningly said.

Flora spent the latter part of the 1960s embroiled in protests against the Vietnam War, and then, progressively, in Women's Liberation, the new feminist movement which had started in America. In 1969, she had met an American woman called Nancy on a feminist anti-war demo, and had fallen deeply in love with her. Feminism said it was okay for women to love women and Flora realized that she had been a lesbian all along. Nancy was dynamic: full of energy and ideas, but an anarchist, and cruel. By Election Night in 1970, Flora is dispirited to think of how much time she spends just worrying about Nancy.

Eileen's career had also taken an erratic turn. Eileen was always passionate about the theatre, but when the affair with the actor turned sour – his wife became pregnant a fourth, and then a fifth, time, despite his oaths that he never made love to her – Eileen became progressively agitated by events in Ireland. She had been present at Burntollet; she had joined the Civil Rights marches which had started seriously in 1968; she was one of Bernadette Devlin's most committed adherents.

Eileen had also become emotionally entangled with a Civil Rights leader who was killed in an accident caused by a drunken Protestant riot on the eve of the Twelfth of July, 1969. This embittered her profoundly.

It was a sweet June evening that year. The four girls were no longer together, yet they thought of one another and that night in 1964, which seemed to be the beginning of their adult lives.

Jocasta remembers to telephone Flora at the flat: the number is now 01-351-2328. But there is no reply. Flora is attending the new review *Oh! Calcutta* and worrying about Nancy. She tries calling Jane and Roy instead. But they have hired a babysitter for the evening while they go to the movies, their enduring pleasure, to see *2001–A Space Odyssey*. Jane actually, is pregnant again. Jocasta tries the last number she had for Eileen, but Eileen is sitting in a pub in Derry, extremely depressed and rather drunk, and even more miserable when she discovers that the Conservatives are likely to get back into Government, led by Ted Heath.

Jocasta's man, Max, celebrates Ted Heath's victory by

buying himself an Alfa Romeo saloon car at the outrageous price of £1,935. (The permissive society!' jokes Max: more VD brings more patients, of course.) But prices are rising generally. Chicken costs three shillings a pound; a house in South Hampstead fetches the astronomical sum of £19,000; a Turner watercolour makes a record £31,000 at auction. And accountants are earning £3,000 a year.

28 February 1974

For Election Night in 1974, Jocasta decides to give a party. She and Max were married in 1971, after she became unexpectedly pregnant. Although an advocate of the Pill, she did not take it herself – 'for health reasons', as she explained, without conscious medical irony. Max dissolved in tears when he heard about the pregnancy, and she hadn't the heart to tell him that she was vacillating over abortion. They got married instead, but as luck would have it, she lost the baby at fifteen weeks, which distressed her more than she could have imagined. Max was overcome with melancholy and cried like a child. He harangued her for not quitting work, but she told him that was nothing to do with it. Jocasta was to have two more miscarriages before giving up hope of a baby. 'Woman proposes, nature disposes,' she remarked ruefully. Choice wasn't as easy as one thought. When she and Max enquired about adoption possibilities, they discovered that legal abortion had cut down drastically on the supply of babies available for adoption.

They were to have a cordial evening, in their St John's Wood flat, which was extremely comfortable. There were more than thirty friends present, including Flora – alone – and Jane with her husband. Flora was rather sad that evening. Her friend Nancy had gone off to Chile on an impulse, had disappeared and was presumed dead. Flora had become quieter, and gloomier. She had taken up social work, after a certain amount of disillusionment with the Trotskyist factions. But the volume of human problems and their extraordinary intractability cast Flora down.

Eileen was absent. Jocasta hadn't heard from her now for nearly three years and the others were out of touch with her too. In fact, Eileen is still in Northern Ireland, deeply mixed up with the fringes of terrorist organizations and the deepening troubles in Northern Ireland. She has more or less given up the theatre and is living on the dole in Derry. The events of Bloody Sunday, when British paratroopers open fire on innocent Catholics and kill thirteen, are shattering to her. They draw her into the Sinn Fein net, and she now hates the Labour party, with a terrible fury, for having sent the troops to Ulster.

Through the network of Marxist contacts, Flora knew what had happened to Eileen, although she did not tell the others. She also knew what kept Eileen away from London these days. After the Guildford bombings – when five people were killed and sixty-five injured in a terrorist attack – anti-Irish feeling had sprung up in England. Flora knew exactly of Eileen's whereabouts; that very election evening, Eileen was with Bridget Rose Dugdale, in a safe house in Dublin. When Harold Wilson won with a tiny majority, Eileen's lip curled dismissively. 'What's the difference,' she said. 'They're all Brits.'

Jocasta's party was held by candle-light because there were power cuts, due to industrial action. 'Your friends the Communist miners,' said Max to Flora, cutting in his bonhomie. His new BMW turbo-charged saloon had just cost him £5,221. The permissive society was yielding ever more VD harvests.

Flora just smiled politely in reply. She knew Max didn't like her, but she was too inherently well-mannered to be personally awkward to her friend's husband.

'I had a bet today,' she said, changing the subject. She knew Max liked a little gamble.

'The road to ruin for you, my dear,' he said handing her a glass of Saumur, which now cost over £2 a bottle. 'You need *judgment* to gamble.'

'It was an irresistible offer, for a feminist,' Flora said, taking the wine. 'Ladbroke's were offering a hundred to one on the former health minister, Margaret Thatcher, becoming Britain's first woman Prime Minister.'

'But she's awful,' Jocasta interjected. 'She cut free milk supplies for schoolchildren. Thatcher – milk snatcher. She may be a woman but she is no friend of the welfare state.'

'I agree she's pretty terrible,' rejoined Flora. 'I just couldn't resist the notion of putting money on a woman.'

'How much?' Max asked.

Flora wouldn't reveal that. It was her secret, she said.

'You're crazy,' he shrugged. 'Barbara Castle is the only woman worth putting money on – she's the only one who has a chance of getting to Number Ten. Maybe Shirley Williams, with very good odds. But a woman leading the *Tories*? Impossible.

'No, the next Conservative PM will be Keith Joseph, believe you me. A Jewish Prime Minister – that's what we'll have.' Max had in fact laid out £500 on Sir Keith's candidature.

Jane and Roy enjoyed the evening especially. They didn't get out a lot nowadays, with three children to worry about. Jane quit teaching after the third; her last school had been, in any case, a handful. She was beginning to wonder, now that her own children were starting education, if comprehensive education was always such a brilliant idea. Roy's business was getting along nicely, and he was branching into the photocopying area. They now lived in Romford, and their old flat in Notting Hill Gate was still occupied by Jane's sister, who had taken up with a Rastafarian and smoked a lot of dope. They are both unemployed, and point to the rising numbers of jobless as a cause. Jane worries about her sister as well as her own children, her husband's business and her ailing mother-in-law. Her taste for responsibility is more than fully satisfied, and as a holiday from such responsibilities she uncharacteristically drinks a tiny bit too much white wine for Election Night.

From China, it is learned that Chairman Mao has had a stroke, and from America, that Senator Edward Kennedy's wife has been charged with drunken driving.

3 May 1979

It is a wonderfully warm May day for the contest between Mr James Callaghan, Prime Minister and leader of the Labour Party, and Mrs Margaret Thatcher, leader of the Opposition and of the Conservative and Unionist Party.

That morning, Eileen was hanging out the family washing in her garden in County Donegal. She had unexpectedly married in 1976. Her husband, Frank O'Donnell, was a calm Donegal teacher and a minor poet, respected in a quiet way without ever being in danger of becoming fashionable. This marriage had had a healing, tranquillizing effect on Eileen, for her life since the early 70s had been turbulent, disordered and without guidance. Eileen was a girl who thought with her heart rather than her head, and needed the ballast of someone like Frank. She still boiled with rage when she thought of the Ulster troubles, but she was beginning to appreciate that there were no easy answers. After the birth of her first child in 1977, she developed a spontaneous revulsion for violence. And by May of 1979, she was pregnant again.

She went inside to make a cup of tea, and on hearing speculation about the British election on the radio, on an impulse she decided to ring Jane. Jane would know what had happened to the others.

Jane picked up the telephone in her kitchen in Essex. She was thrilled to hear from Eileen, although they had begun sending Christmas cards again and she knew of Eileen's marriage. Jane tells her the news. She has some family problems – her second son, James, has 'school phobia', that is, an exaggerated dread of going to school, and is into therapy sessions with an educational psychologist. Jane suspects that the real problem is old-fashioned bullying and poor school management. Her youngest child, a girl, Lucinda, has had an operation for a hole in the heart and is still on the delicate side. Meanwhile, Jane tells her friend, Jocasta has had an operation for cancer. Yes, she was showing some women how to examine their breasts when she detected a lump in her own. This was only last year –

1978. In consequence, she has had a radical mastectomy, at the age of thirty-eight. Poor Jocasta. Max has been superbly supportive, although the marriage, like all marriages – Jane adds – has gone through its rocky phases.

As for Flora, Jane says, she is working in a hostel for the homeless in Piccadilly. She had been extremely depressed when it was confirmed that her friend Nancy had indeed been murdered in Chile by fascist forces. Nancy had been a pain in the neck, in Jane's opinion. She used to go and steal from the local Indian shops in West London, on the grounds that small shopkeepers were 'economic fascists'. Poor Mr and Mrs Patel, who got up early in the morning to earn their living, were the object of this woman's daft politics! Really!

'You'll be voting for Mrs Thatcher next,' teased Eileen.

'I'll be voting for her today,' rejoined Jane. 'It's exactly what this country needs! You should talk to Roy about the trade unions!'

Eileen was flabbergasted. She couldn't believe that someone of her generation would vote Tory. But of course they were all in their mid-thirties by now, growing middle-aged, and Jane, in particular, was more concerned with her children than with political analysis, thought Eileen.

As Mrs Thatcher enters Downing Street, sanctimoniously quoting St Francis of Assisi, a generation of Labour voters feel defeated; some have grown disillusioned, of course, and some have just grown old.

Max buys himself a new BMW, which costs £7,299. Flora, who hasn't bothered to vote (though she toyed with supporting the Ecology Party), realizes that her bet on Margaret Thatcher will bring her winnings of £100,000. Not that she needs it.

9 June 1983

Thursday was always a good day for shopping in London, and Jane decided that she would make a day of it. Then she realized it was election day and her thoughts turned to the old gang of friends. Life was so busy nowadays, there never seemed time to

see people. There was always something to do for the children –
take them to the dentist, fit them for new clothes, see their
teachers, take Lucinda to the hospital. And then Jane was
involved with a local Meals on Wheels group which helped care
for the elderly, she was a governor of a nearby school and she
had been invited to become a JP. Still, she dropped a card to
Jocasta and asked her for lunch at the University Women's
Club in South Audley Street. Jocasta was a busy consultant
now, but she might welcome the chance for lunch and a gossip.

Jane noticed, as Jocasta arrived, how her friend had aged.
Well, Jocasta was over forty now, and she had survived the
cancer. Yes, Jocasta told her over lunch, triumphant but grim,
she had survived the vital five years and she was determined to
survive the next. But her marriage had gone bust. Jane was
flabbergasted. Why, Max had seemed so strong and sweet over
the various problems . . .

'Yes, but his life has fallen apart,' said Jocasta, sipping soup.
'Have you heard about AIDS?'

'Something vague,' Jane said, thinking. 'Something in
America, is it?'

'It's a time-bomb. Max noticed, about two years ago, that
there was another big increase in his VD patients. VD has
been increasing perceptively over the years and Max has never
been alarmist about that. You know how he used to rub his
hands in mock-glee and exclaim "the harvest of the permissive
society" '?

Jane remembered Max's self-consciously hammy jokes
along these lines.

'It's not at all funny any more. AIDS is a fatal disease, spread
by promiscuity and drug-abuse. Max just cannot face the fact
that patients of his are *dying*. The reason that he liked ordinary
VD practice was that he cured everyone. He always made that
Marilyn Monroe joke – do you remember? "Sex never gave
anyone cancer." Well, now it does. Kaposi's sarcoma is one of
the recognizable outcomes of being HIV positive.'

Jane didn't follow everything that Jocasta was saying: all
this was new information to her. But she was shocked enough.

'Max went into a deep depression after he treated a child for AIDS. The child is now dying. You know how sentimental Max is about children; he took the miscarriages worse than me, really. He more or less had a breakdown. The child got AIDS, by the way, by inheriting it from her mother. The sins of the fathers shall be visited on the children, eh?'

'It's amazing,' said Jane, shaking her head. 'How hard it is to get rid of all the old rules. They come back again and again.'

Jocasta looked melancholic. 'We will cure AIDS,' she affirmed her faith in science. 'But not for a long while. And not in time to save my marriage to Max. Jane, I just can't cope with the moroseness, the weeping, the way he is forever on the point of cracking up. *And* he's into some kind of remorse, as though he feels he encouraged people to screw around by making light of it.'

'Poor Max,' said Jane softly. 'And poor you.'

'Still,' Jocasta went on. 'In other ways, I suppose things are okay. My sister has had her fourth baby, which is nice. Eileen is a lot happier than she used to be; her husband seems to be a really nice man, and she's getting back a bit into acting work again now that her kids are no longer babies. And you know what's happened to Flora? Oh, my dear, the 180-degree turnaround. She has now taken up religion and has gone off on a Christian Aid mission to the Third World. Her half-brother and his live-in girlfriend have the Earl's Court flat now. I believe she's divested herself of almost all her assets and given them away to Third World charities.'

'I thought,' said Jane, smiling, 'that she would finally come to the view that charity didn't necessarily perpetuate capitalism, or at least if it did, that was not the important point about it. Flora is too genuinely good a person to be satisfied by politics, I believe. I wonder if she has found someone to share her life?'

Jocasta hadn't heard. She looked at her watch. She had to return to the clinic; it was her afternoon for talking to older mothers about the results of their amniocenteses, and there was one with bad news on the way – a stinker of an inherited disease called Duchenne's Syndrome. The advances in knowledge about pregnancy had been huge in recent years, though Jocasta occasionally caught herself thinking an unscientific thought from the Book of Ecclesiastes: 'In greater knowledge is greater sorrow.'

'Don't forget to vote!' she bid Jane goodbye with a kiss. Jane smiled a fond farewell: it was so nice to hear about old friends, such a comfort in all the anxieties of her age, when a woman has so many responsibilities to the younger family, and to the older members too. Roy's elderly mother was soon to move in with them; Jane had volunteered to care for her.

But before she took the train back to Essex, she visited Harrods and went to the movies, indulging herself in the marvellously escapist world of the latest release, *Murder on the Orient Express*.

11 June 1987

Picture, if you will, a roomy, well-appointed flat in Hampstead, north London. The year is 1987. Pictures of cats by Lesley-Anne Ivory adorn the walls, as does a tear-sheet from the *Independent* newspaper on the healthy habit of polyunsaturates. There is also a cutting from the *Daily Express*: 'Don't Sleep Around, Girls, says Top Doc.' Jocasta has recently given a paper on the dangers of too much early sexual activity, and of too many partners, for young girls.

It is polling day, once more. Twenty-three years after their first Election Night party, Jocasta has decided to try and get the four former flat-mates together again. She is not sure if they can all turn up. But she hopes for the best.

She knows that life has been very demanding for Jane. Her mother-in-law had become senile in her care, and Jane was selfless in her devotion to the old lady. Her middle son, James, who had never been easy, developed a drug problem, although, thankfully, he did not inject. Her daughter's health remained a cause for concern. Still, Roy's business was booming, and when they sold their little Notting Hill flat in 1986 – Jane's sister was now a single mum with two children, and had found suitable council housing at last – it fetched £187,000. As Jocasta cooled the champagne and prepared the *canapés*, she thought to herself – 'I do hope Jane can come. She so enjoys a night out, and she does deserve it.'

There was a good chance she would. And there was every reason to hope that Eileen would make it too. Eileen now lived at Edgebaston, near Birmingham, where Frank had become a lecturer in poetry and literature at the polytechnic. Jocasta had seen Eileen the previous November – Eileen had been in London doing a BBC play reading and they had had tea at the Reform Club, which had recently started admitting lady members. Eileen was stouter now, and her rich dark hair had skeins of grey, but there was a mature calmness about her that Jocasta found reassuring. She couldn't help hearing mutterings in her sub-conscious about the healing effects of the love of a good man.

As Jocasta took the salmon *en croûte* (straight from Marks & Spencer's, for nowadays it was the fashion to admit that M & S was your chef) from the fridge, she hoped that Max would pop around later too – thinking, she smiled, of the love of a good man. They no longer lived together, but their relationship, of late, had become cordial.

The real question-mark hung over Flora. Extraordinarily, Flora was in Britain. She had flown back from Ethiopia a week ago – where she was working on a famine relief project – because her Scottish grandmother was dying. Jocasta had seen the death announced in *The Times*, and sent a card to the old address. Flora had phoned her from Scotland in response and promised she would try to make it, for old times sake. She sounded so much more cheerful than she had been in the 1970s, notwithstanding the funereal circumstances of her trip back. But then Lady Gordon had reached ninety and had enjoyed a good innings. It occurred to Jocasta that Flora would probably be Lady Gordon's principal beneficiary, as she had always had a special relationship with the doughty old Suffragette.

Despite her Francis of Assisi gestures, Flora would probably once again be very rich, as Lady Gordon had substantial banking and insurance interests in Hong Kong and there were no other direct descendants. Funny, thought Jocasta: despite her repudiation of money, Flora can't help getting it. Some people are like that, and some people are not. Jocasta's belief in man – and especially woman – being in control of destiny was constantly modified these days by observations about luck, timing, chance and the way things are.

The front door-bell rang. It was Jane, with Eileen. They had met on the doorstep and came in together, laughing very merrily. They kissed Jocasta warmly, thrusting more bottles into her hands.

'Oh girls, girls!' Jocasta protested.

'Do you remember the bottle of wine we shared together in – wasn't it 1964?' Jane asked. 'It was plonk, for ten and six from the Chelsea wine store. That was about four per cent of a secretary's salary. Today, champagne is £7 in Sainsbury's. That is only about five per cent of a secretary's salary today.'

'Thatcher's Britain,' mused Jocasta. 'People are driven to drink. With the cuts in the National Health Service, I'm not surprised.' Jocasta had been an SDP voter of late.

'And my cigarettes were four shillings – and they're now £1.86,' remarked Eileen, not wishing to be drawn into discussions about Thatcher's Britain. She admired Mrs Thatcher for having the bottle to sign the Anglo-Irish Treaty in the face of Ulster Unionist opposition, but that was as far as she would go, publicly.

'And you shouldn't still be smoking them!' Jocasta admonished. Like all doctors at the time, she had become rabid about anti-smoking.

'Well, here's to us, ladies!' Jane lifted her glass. 'We've survived!'

'We've survived!' echoed Jocasta, thinking that for her, it had sometimes seemed like a close-run thing.

The women, now all well into their forties, set about putting the last garnishings on the food, and helping themselves liberally to the champagne. Jane and Eileen's husbands would join them presently, and Max might drop by as well.

They were watching David Dimbleby on television saying that although a Thatcher win was expected, a late Labour resurgence was still possible, when the doorbell went again. Jocasta pressed the entryphone button and went out on the staircase. They could hear voices and kisses being exchanged, and little shrieks of amazement and amicability.

Flora appeared, brown with the Africa sun. She had a child of about five by her side, very gorgeous and black, with the most wonderful large eyes. 'My son,' she beamed. 'My adopted son.' The child smiled, turned bashful, and clung to her trousered leg. Flora had never looked happier. She had at last found a real cause: a person. Eileen could see straight away that this, at last, was something Flora could care about, lastingly. Eileen felt overcome at the sight of gangley Flora, all legs and arms, with this adorable little boy.

'It's lovely to see you all, really wonderful,' Flora said, with feeling. And there were more warm embracings. Jocasta thrust a glass into Flora's hands and they all four laughed as little Josef stretched his tiny hand up for a taste.

On BBC TV, it was announced that Margaret Thatcher would be Prime Minister for a third term.

'I voted for her,' said Jane. 'But who cares about politics?'

Jane was the only one of the four to admit openly that she had travelled the road that led to a vote for Margaret Thatcher: age; realism; disillusion with Utopia; experience.

'It's people that count, not politics; believe me,' said Flora with conviction, as she started to talk about her African experiences.

Max was on his way to join the ladies in his new Saab *coupé*, which he had bought to cheer himself up after an AIDS conference in Atlanta. For £24,000. At auction, a picture of Van Gogh's fetched £22 million.